A RIGHT TO DIE

OTHER BOOKS BY REX STOUT

Novels

HOW LIKE A GOD · GOLDEN REMEDY · SEED ON THE WIND
O CARELESS LOVE! · MR. CINDERELLA · FOREST FIRE
THE PRESIDENT VANISHES

Nero Wolfe Mysteries

FER-DE-LANCE · THE LEAGUE OF FRIGHTENED MEN
THE RUBBER BAND · THE RED BOX · SOME BURIED CAESAR
OVER MY DEAD BODY · BLACK ORCHIDS
WHERE THERE'S A WILL · NOT QUITE DEAD ENOUGH
TOO MANY COOKS · THE SILENT SPEAKER
TOO MANY WOMEN · AND BE A VILLAIN
TROUBLE IN TRIPLICATE · THE SECOND CONFESSION
THREE DOORS TO DEATH · IN THE BEST FAMILIES
CURTAINS FOR THREE · MURDER BY THE BOOK
TRIPLE JEOPARDY · PRISONER'S BASE · THE GOLDEN SPIDERS
THREE MEN OUT · THE BLACK MOUNTAIN
FULL HOUSE: A NERO WOLFE OMNIBUS · BEFORE MIDNIGHT
THREE WITNESSES · MIGHT AS WELL BE DEAD
THREE FOR THE CHAIR · IF DEATH EVER SLEPT
AND FOUR TO GO · ALL ACES: A NERO WOLFE OMNIBUS
CHAMPAGNE FOR ONE · PLOT IT YOURSELF
THREE AT WOLFE'S DOOR · TOO MANY CLIENTS
FIVE OF A KIND: THE THIRD NERO WOLFE OMNIBUS
HOMICIDE TRINITY: A NERO WOLFE THREESOME
THE FINAL DEDUCTION · GAMBIT · THE MOTHER HUNT
TRIO FOR BLUNT INSTRUMENTS

Tecumseh Fox Mysteries

DOUBLE FOR DEATH · THE BROKEN VASE · BAD FOR BUSINESS

Mysteries

THE HAND IN THE GLOVE · MOUNTAIN CAT
ALPHABET HICKS · RED THREADS

A Right to Die

A NERO WOLFE NOVEL

Rex Stout

New York • *The Viking Press*

Second printing November 1964

Copyright © 1964 by Rex Stout

All rights reserved

First published in 1964 by The Viking Press, Inc.
625 Madison Avenue, New York, N.Y. 10022

Published simultaneously in Canada by
The Macmillan Company of Canada Limited

Library of Congress catalog card number: 64–22621
Printed in U.S.A. by The Colonial Press

A RIGHT TO DIE

1

He had no appointment and, looking at him across the door-sill, it didn't seem likely that he would be bringing the first big fee of 1964. But when he said his name was Whipple and he wanted to consult Mr. Wolfe I let him in and took him to the office, because after a long dull day I would welcome Wolfe's glare at me for breaking a rule, and also because he was a Negro. So far as I knew, in their hot campaign for civil rights the Negroes hadn't mentioned the right to consult a private detective, but why not? So I didn't even ask him what the trouble was. In the office, when I put him in the red leather chair near the end of Wolfe's desk, he looked around and then leaned back and closed his eyes. I had told him that Wolfe would be down in ten minutes, at six o'clock, and he had nodded and said, "I know. Orchids."

Sitting at my desk, I swiveled when the sound came of the elevator and was facing the door when Wolfe entered. When he was in far enough to see the man in the chair he stopped and turned to me, and the glare was one of his best. I met it square.

"Mr. Whipple," I said. "To consult you."

He held the glare. He was deciding whether to turn and march out, to the kitchen, or to bellow. But suddenly the glare became a frown, and he said, not a bellow, "Whipple?"

"Yes, sir."

He wheeled for a look at the man, circled around his desk to his outsize chair, sat, and aimed the frown at the man. "Well, sir?"

The man smiled a little and said, "I'm going to make a speech." He cleared his throat and cocked his head. "The agreements of human society embrace not only protection against murder, but thousands of other things, and it is certainly true that in America the whites have excluded the blacks from some of the benefits of those agreements. It is said that the exclusion has sometimes even extended to murder—that in parts of this country a white man may kill a black one, if not with impunity, at least with a good chance of escaping the penalty which the agreement imposes. That's deplorable, and I don't blame black men for resenting it. But how do you propose to change it?"

He turned a hand over. "I'll skip a little. But if you shield him because he is your color there is a great deal to say. You are rendering your race a serious disservice. You are helping to perpetuate and aggravate the very exclusions which you justly resent. The ideal human agreement is one in which distinctions of race and color and religion are totally disregarded; anyone helping to preserve those distinctions is postponing that ideal; and you are certainly helping to preserve them. If

in a question of murder you permit your action to be in-
fluenced . . ."

He went on, but I wasn't listening. My eyes were at him,
but I wasn't seeing him. I was seeing a room in the Upshur
Pavilion at Kanawha Spa, West Virginia, as it had been late
one night many years ago. Wolfe was on a chair not big enough
for his seventh of a ton, facing an audience of fourteen colored
men, cooks and waiters, seated on the floor. He knew, and so
did I, that one of them had a vital piece of information regarding a murder, and for two hours he had been trying to find
out which one, with no success. Around two a.m. he tried
another angle and made a long speech, and that did it. It
loosened up a twenty-one-year-old college boy, Howard University, named Paul Whipple, and he blurted it out. And the
man in the red leather chair was delivering, word for word,
parts of the speech Wolfe had made that long-ago night.

I left Upshur Pavilion and came back to what I was looking
at. Should I have recognized him? No. Then he had been
young and slim with no extra meat on his face muscles; now
he was middle-aged, going bald, with saggy cheeks, wearing
cheaters with black rims. But the name, Whipple, should have
rung a bell, and it hadn't. It had for Wolfe. I did not like that.
I will concede that he is a genius and I am not, but on memory
I'll concede nothing.

He stopped—in the middle of a sentence, because that was
where he had interrupted Wolfe that night. He glanced at
me with a little smile, settled back in the chair, and shifted the
smile to Wolfe.

Wolfe grunted. "You have a good memory, Mr. Whipple."

He shook his head. "Not really. Not usually. But that speech
was a high spot in my education. I wrote it down that night.

If I had a good memory I could do a better job at my work."

"What is your work?"

"I'm a teacher, an assistant professor at Columbia. I'm afraid I'll never move up."

"Anthropology?"

Whipple's eyes widened. "Good lord, talk about memory. You remember *that*?"

"Certainly. You mentioned it." Wolfe's lips puckered. "You have me cornered, sir. I know I am beholden to you. But for you I might have been stuck there for days—weeks. And of course you have tickled my vanity, quoting me verbatim at length. So you need me for something?"

Whipple nodded. "That's putting it bluntly, but I know you're always blunt. Yes, I need you." He smiled, more of a smile than before. "I need help on a very confidential matter, and I decided to come to you. I doubt if I can pay what you would normally charge, but I can pay."

"That can wait. I have said I have an obligation. Your problem?"

"It's very . . . personal." His lips worked. He looked at me and back at Wolfe. "In a way, it's related to what you said that night; that's why I quoted it. I have a son, Dunbar, twenty-three years old. Do you remember that you quoted Paul Laurence Dunbar that night?"

"Certainly."

"Well, we named our son Dunbar. He's a good enough boy. He has his share of shortcomings, but on the whole he's a pretty good boy. He works for the ROCC. Do you know what the ROCC is?"

Wolfe nodded. "The Rights of Citizens Committee. I have sent them small contributions."

"Why?"

A corner of Wolfe's mouth went up. "Come, Mr. Whipple. Another speech to quote?"

"I could use one, or my people could. My son could. He's pretty good at a speech. But he's what I—he's the problem, or rather, he's *in* the problem. He has got involved with a white girl and he's going to marry her, and I can't talk him out of it. So I need help."

Wolfe made a face. "Not mine," he said emphatically.

Whipple shook his head. "Not to talk to him. To find out what's wrong with her."

"Except for the innate and universal flaws of her sex, there may be nothing wrong with her."

"But obviously there is." His brows were up. "She is—not speaking as an anthropologist—of good family. She is young, attractive, and financially independent. For her to marry a Negro is absurd. Obviously—"

"My dear sir. Instead of another speech I could quote for an hour. Benjamin Franklin: 'A man in a passion rides a wild horse.' Or, by courtesy, a woman. An ancient Latin proverb: '*Ex visu amor.*' Loving comes by looking. Pfui. Nothing in nature is absurd, though much is deplorable."

"That's irrelevant."

"Indeed?"

"Yes." Whipple smiled. "Do you remember that when you asked me how old I was and I said twenty-one, Moulton told me to say 'Sir'? Passion or love is not the point. A white woman taking to a black man, even going to bed with him, there's nothing absurd about that. But not marriage. I say if this Susan Brooke wants to marry my son there's something wrong with her. She has a screw loose. All the difficulties, the snags, the embarrassments, the complications . . . I don't need to list them for you."

"No."

"She couldn't possibly be a good wife to him, and she ought to know it. There's something wrong with her. It may be something specific in her past, or it may be her basic character. If I can find out what it is I can put it up to my son; he's not a fool. But the finding out—I don't know how, I'm not equipped for it. But you are." He turned his palms up. "So here I am."

Wolfe said distinctly, "Pride of race."

"What! Who?"

"You, of course. You may not be aware—"

Whipple was moving, up. On his feet, his eyes, half closed, slanted down at Wolfe. "I am not a racist. I see I have made a mistake. I didn't think—"

"Nonsense. Sit down. Your problem—"

"Forget it. Forget me. I should have forgotten you. To accuse me of—"

"Confound it," Wolfe bellowed, "sit down! An anthropologist disclaiming pride of race? You should know better. If you are an anthropos you have it. The remark was not offensive, but I withdraw it because it was pointless. You have been moved to action; what moved you is immaterial. What moves me is the fact that I'm indebted to you and you have dunned me, and I'll pay. But first I have a comment. Will you please sit down?"

"I suppose I'm touchy," Whipple said, and sat.

Wolfe regarded him. "The comment is about marriage. It's possible that Miss Brooke is more realistic than you are. She may be intelligent enough to know that no matter whom she marries there will be the devil to pay. The difficulties, snags, embarrassments, and complications—I use your words, though I would prefer sharper ones—are in any case inevitable. If she marries a man of her own color and class, the grounds for them will be paltry, ignoble, degrading, and tiresome. If she

marries a Negro the grounds will be weighty, worthy, conse-
quential, and diverting. I have never met a woman with so
much sense, but there may be one. What if it is Miss Brooke?"

Whipple was shaking his head. "No, sir. Of course that's
very clever. It's good talk, but it's talk." He smiled. "My father used to say about a good talker, 'He rides words bare-
back.' No, sir."

"You're fixed."

"Yes. If you want to put it that way, I am."

"Very well. You remember Mr. Goodwin."

Whipple shot me a glance. "Of course."

"Will you arrange for him to meet Miss Brooke? Perhaps a
meal, lunch or dinner, with you, her, and your son? With
some plausible pretext?"

He was looking doubtful. "I'm afraid that isn't possible. She
knows what I—my attitude. Does Mr. Goodwin have to meet
her? And my son?"

"Not necessarily your son. Her, yes. I can't proceed until
he has seen her, spoken with her, and if possible danced with
her, and reported. That may even settle it. His feeling for
attractive young women, his understanding of them, and his
talent for gaining their confidence may be all we'll need." He
turned. "Archie. Have you a suggestion?"

I nodded. "Sure." He had asked for it. "I meet her, feel her
out, understand her, get her confidence, bring her here and
install her in the south room, and you seduce her and then
marry her. As for the difficulties, snags, embar—"

Whipple cut in. "Mr. Goodwin. You can joke about it, but
I can't."

I met his eyes. "I wouldn't expect you to, Mr. Whipple. I
was merely reacting to Mr. Wolfe's joke about me and attractive young women. But of course I'll have to meet her. He

never leaves the house on business. How urgent is it? Have they set a date for the wedding?"

"No."

"How sure are you they're not already married?"

"I'm quite sure. My son wouldn't do that. He wouldn't dissemble with me—or with his mother."

"Is his mother with you on this?"

"Yes. Completely." He turned to Wolfe. "You said your remark about pride of race was pointless, but you had made the remark. With my wife I suppose it could be called that. Is it pride of race if she wants her son's wife to be a girl, a woman, with whom she can be friends? *Real* friends? Speaking as an American Negro, as a man, and as an anthropologist, can she expect to get true familial intimacy from a white woman?"

"No," Wolfe said. "Nor from a colored woman either if it's her son's wife." He waved it away. "However, you're fixed." He tilted his head to look at the wall clock: forty minutes till dinner. "Since Mr. Goodwin's suggestion isn't feasible, let's see if we can find one. Tell me all you know about Miss Brooke."

I got out my notebook.

It took only half an hour, so there were still ten minutes when I returned to the office after escorting Whipple to the front, helping him on with his coat, handing him his hat, and letting him out. Wolfe sat with his current book, closed, in his hands, gazing at it with his lips tight. He had been cheated out of a full hour of reading.

I stood and looked down at him. "If you expect an apology," I said, "you'll have to expect. When you make personal remarks about me with company present, I react."

His head came up. "Of course. You always do. I'm in the middle of a chapter."

"I didn't know that. As for my letting him in and not telling you, there are exceptions to—"

"Bah. You wanted to see if I would recognize him. I didn't until I heard the name. Did you?"

"Since we're being frank, no. Not his face or voice. With me too it was the name." I went on. It's better to keep going after a lie. "Anyway, it's a new slant on civil rights. She has a right to marry the man she loves, and look who's trying to stop her. He had a nerve to begin by quoting that speech."

He grunted. "I'm obliged."

"Yeah. We're really going to tackle it?"

"You are."

"You leave it to me?"

"No. We'll discuss it later."

"There isn't much to discuss. No matter what we dig up about her, he'll probably—"

There were footsteps in the hall, and Fritz was at the door to announce dinner. Wolfe put the book down, stroked it with his fingertips, and rose.

2

That was Monday, February 24. Forty-two hours later, at one o'clock Wednesday, I had lunch with Susan Brooke at Lily Rowan's penthouse on 63rd Street between Madison and Park.

In the random assortment of facts Whipple had supplied there had been nothing to bite on. She had graduated from Radcliffe four or five years ago, and not long after had come to New York. She was living with her married brother, an electronics engineer, in his Park Avenue apartment, and so was her mother. They were from Wisconsin—Racine, Whipple thought, but wasn't sure. He didn't actually know that she was financially independent; he had assumed it, because for more than two years she had been working for the ROCC as a volunteer, no pay, and she had made cash contributions amounting to $2350. Not office work; she made contacts and arranged fund-raising parties and meetings.

That was about all Whipple knew, except for a couple of

dozen useless little details and a few even more useless guesses.

The Lily Rowan idea was of course mine, since she was my friend, not Wolfe's. My first suggestion, Monday evening after dinner, was that I would phone the ROCC office, speak with the executive director, Thomas Henchy, and tell him that Wolfe was considering making a substantial contribution, that he would like to discuss it, and that in my opinion the best person to send to see him would be Miss Susan Brooke because I had heard that she made a good impression with men. That was vetoed by Wolfe on the ground (a) that he would feel committed to a substantial contribution, at least a grand, and (b) that with an attractive young woman I would get farther sooner if he wasn't present. Of course the real ground was that she was a woman. There are many things he likes about the old brownstone on West 35th Street, which he owns: the furniture and rugs and books and soundproofing; the plant rooms on the roof; Fritz Brenner, the chef; the big kitchen; Theodore Horstmann, the orchid nurse; and me, the man and the muscle. But what he likes best is that there is no woman in it, and it would suit him fine if one never crossed the doorsill.

So I suggested Lily Rowan, to whom a grand is peanuts, and that was satisfactory. When I rang her, that evening, she said she didn't like to discuss dirty work on the phone so I had better come in person, and I went, and got back to 35th Street and to bed at a quarter past two. Since I take a full eight hours short of murder, I didn't get to the office Tuesday morning until after Wolfe had come down from his two hours in the plant rooms—nine to eleven. Around noon Lily phoned. Miss Brooke would be there tomorrow for lunch at one o'clock, and I might come earlier for more briefing.

The two miles crosstown and up to 63rd Street is one of my favorite walks, but that Wednesday it took plenty of man and muscle. When it's twenty above and at every corner a snowy blast that has been practicing ever since it left Hudson Bay lowers your chin and clamps your mouth shut and bends you nearly double, you have to grit your teeth to go on by all the handy doors to shops and bars and hotel lobbies. When I finally made it, shook the snow off of my coat and hat under the canopy and in the lobby, took the elevator and left it at the top and pushed the button, and Lily opened the door, I said, "The nearest bed."

She raised a brow, a trick I taught her. "Try next door," she said. She let me by and shut the door. "You didn't *walk*!"

"Sure. You could call it walking." I put my hat and coat in the closet. "If they walked up Everest, I walked here."

We linked arms and entered the living room, with its 19-by-34 Kashan rug, a garden pattern in seven colors, its Renoir and Manet and Cézanne, its off-white piano, and its glass doors to the terrace, where the wind was giving the snow a big play. When we sat she poked her feet out, the shins parallel, and muttered, "Antelope legs."

"In the first place," I said, "that was many years ago. In the second place, what I said was that you looked like an antelope in a herd of Guernseys. In a crowd you still do. We will now discuss Miss Brooke, though she probably won't make it in this weather."

But she did, only ten minutes late. Lily let the maid admit her but met her at the arch to the foyer. I stood in the middle of the Kashan and was introduced as Mr. Goodwin, her business adviser.

The description that Whipple had given us of her had been biased. She wasn't skinny. She was small, a couple of inches shorter than Lily, who came up to my nose, with smooth fair skin, brown hair and eyes, and hardly any lipstick on her wide full mouth. Her handshake was firm and friendly without over-doing it. Lily told me afterward that her brown woolen dress was probably Bergdorf, two hundred bucks. She didn't want a cocktail.

I left it to Lily. At lunch—mushroom chowder, lobster souf-flé, avocado salad, pineapple mousse—she stuck to ROCC: people, record, policy, program. Susan Brooke knew it all and knew how to tell it. It was a good pitch for almost anybody this side of Governor Wallace or Senator Eastland.

The question whether Lily should give her a check or stall was for Lily to decide, but the further question, whether to give it to her before getting personal or after, had been left to me. Lily made her decision before we left the table; she rubbed her eye with her middle finger. Yes, on the check. I consid-ered my question. Would she be a better quiz prospect while she was still wondering if she had made a sale, or after it was in the bag? My understanding of attractive young women wouldn't tell me, so I fingered in my pocket for a quarter, slipped it out, and glanced at it. Heads. I rubbed my left eye and saw that Lily got it.

Back in the living room, when coffee had been poured, Lily excused herself and left us. In a minute she returned, went to Miss Brooke, and handed her a little rectangle of blue pa-per. "There," she said. "It won't get me into heaven, but it may help a little. Green pastures."

Susan Brooke looked at it—not just a glance, a full look. "The lovely lunch and this too," she said. She had a nice soft voice but ran her words together some. "Many-many thanks, Miss Rowan, but of course they're not just from me, they're from all of us. Is it all right to list you as a patron?"

Lily sat. "Certainly, if you want to. My father made that money building sewers with one hand and playing politics with the other." She picked up her coffee cup and sipped. "Since you can afford to donate your time, I suppose your father knows how to make money too."

"Yes, he did." She closed her bag with the check inside. "Not building sewers, real estate. He died six years ago."

"In New York?"

"No, Wisconsin."

"Oh. Omaha?"

Lily was showing me how smart she was. We had driven across Nebraska on the way to Montana. Miss Brooke politely didn't smile. "No, Racine," she said.

Lily sipped coffee. "I suppose I'm being nosy, but to me it's —well, you're fascinating. I'm not lazy or stingy, I'm merely useless. I simply don't understand you. Do you mind if I try to?"

"No, of course not." She tapped her bag. "Your money isn't useless, Miss Rowan."

Lily flipped a hand. "Tax-deductible. But your time and energy aren't. Have you been doing this ever since you came to New York?"

"Oh no. Only two years—a little more. There's nothing fascinating about me, believe me. When I finished college—I barely made it, I'm Radcliffe 'fifty-nine—I went home to Racine and got good and bored. Then something happened, and— Anyway, my father was dead and only my mother and me in a big house, and we came to New York. My brother was here and he suggested it. But you didn't ask for my autobiography."

"Yes, I did. Practically. You live with your brother?"

She shook her head. "We did for a while, but then we took an apartment—my mother and I. And I got a job." She put her empty cup down, and I got up and filled it. I was glad of the chance to contribute something.

"If you can stand any more," Lily said, "what kind of a job?"

"I can stand it if you can. Reading manuscripts for a publisher. It was terrible—you would never believe what some people think is fit to print. Then I got a job at the UN, a desk job. The job was about as bad, but I met a lot of different people, and I realized how silly I was to do dull paying jobs when I didn't need the pay. It was a girl I met at the UN, a colored girl, who gave me the idea of the ROCC, and I went and asked if I could do something." She drank coffee.

"Absolutely fascinating," Lily declared. "Don't you think so, Mr. Goodwin?"

"No," I said flatly. A business adviser should be tough. "It depends on what satisfies a person, that's all. You ladies both have all the money you need, and in my opinion you're both rather selfish. You could make a couple of men secure and happy and comfortable, but you won't take the trouble. Neither of you is married. At least—you haven't been married, Miss Brooke?"

"No."

"And don't intend to be?"

She laughed, a soft little laugh. "Maybe I will. After what you've said, I'll feel selfish if I don't. I'll invite you and Miss Rowan to the wedding."

"I'll accept with pleasure. By the way, which publisher did you read manuscripts for? I had one rejected once, and it may have been you."

"Oh, I hope not. The Parthenon Press."

"Then it wasn't you. Another by the way, this will amuse you. When Miss Rowan got the idea of making a contribution to the ROCC she asked me to check a little, and I asked around, and one man said there was probably some Communist influence. Of course people say that about any outfit they don't like, but he mentioned a name. Dunbar Whipple. He had no evidence, just hearsay. But Whipple might like to know about it. I'd rather not name the man who said it."

No flush or fluster. She even looked a little amused. "I hope," she said, "this isn't a new way of asking me if I'm a Communist."

"It isn't. I'm plain and simple. I would just say, are you?"

"And I would just say no. At first, when people tried to ask me if I was a Communist without really asking it I got indignant, but I soon saw that was silly. I handle it better now. Are you a Birchite, Mr. Goodwin?"

"I refuse to answer. I'm indignant."

She laughed a little. "You'll get over it. As for Dunbar Whipple, he's special. He's young and he has a lot to learn, but he'll be the first Negro mayor of New York City." She turned. "I warn you, Miss Rowan, some day I may ask you for a different kind of contribution—to the Whipple for Mayor campaign fund. Would you vote for a Negro?"

Lily said it would depend, that she voted for Democrats only, in respect to the memory of her father. I arose to pour coffee, but Miss Brooke looked at her watch and said she had an appointment. Lily gestured toward the terrace and said it was a day to ignore appointments, but Miss Brooke said she couldn't, it was a meeting about a school boycott. She gave Lily a healthy thank-you handshake, but not me, which was proper, since I hadn't said definitely that I wasn't a Birchite. As Lily convoyed her to the foyer I filled my cup and took it to the glass doors to admire the weather.

Lily came to join me. "Quite a gal," she said. "Fighting her way through that to talk school boycott. If she's fascinating, it's lucky for me I'm not."

"It's one of your best points," I said, "that you're not fascinating." I put the cup on a plant stand.

"And that I'm rather selfish. Look me in the eye, Escamillo. Take that back about making you secure and happy and comfortable."

"Not me. I merely said a man."

"Name one."

"Nero Wolfe."

"Ha. What will you bet I couldn't?"

"Not a dime. I know him, but I know you too. No bet."

"You would have to move out." She had a look in her eye, I would say the look of a tiger stalking a herd of deer if I had ever seen a tiger stalk deer. "We would fire Fritz, and of course Theodore. He would read aloud to me. We would ditch the orchids and take out the partitions in the plant rooms and have dancing parties, and you wouldn't be invited. For lunch we would have peanut-butter-and-jelly sandwiches, and—"

I clapped a palm over her mouth with my other hand at the back of her head. With no effort to break away, she tried to bite. I said, "When you're ready to discuss the subject, shut your right eye."

She shut her right eye, and I took my hands away. "Well?"

"I stand pat," she said. "She's fascinating."

"To you. It's perfectly simple. She's a status-seeker. She wants to be the mayor's wife."

"Uhuh. I always laugh at your cracks to make you secure and happy and comfortable, but may I skip that one? You're trying to get something on her that will keep that colored man from marrying her. Right?"

"That's the idea."

"Then two things. First, I don't think you'll get anything unless you invent it, and I know you wouldn't. I don't think there's anything to get—anything bad enough to count. Second, if there is, I hope you don't get it through anything you heard here. I couldn't blame you, but I would blame me. If she and that Negro want to get married they may be darned fools, of course I think they are, but it's their lookout. So do me a favor. If you stop it, and something you heard here got you started on what stops it, don't tell me. I don't want to know. That's me. You know?"

"Sure." I looked at my wrist: a quarter to three. "If I had any personal feelings about it they would be about the same as yours, but I haven't. Rights all over the place. She has a right to marry him. He has a right to marry her. The father and mother have a right to butt in, they've been doing it for ten thousand years. Nero Wolfe has a right to meet an obligation to a man. I have a right to earn my pay by doing what I'm told, providing it doesn't clash with my right to stay out of jail. So I'll run along and drop in at the office of the Parthenon Press, which is only a few blocks from here."

"There won't be anyone there. Look at that snow. I can beat you at gin. Don't they send people home?"

I looked. "They might at that. May I use the phone?"

She was right. I got an answer, but not from the switchboard girl. Some man told me that everybody had gone. When I hung up Lily called through an open door, "I'm in here. Come on. I have a right to win enough to pay for the lunch."

She did, about.

3

That was a new experience. Over the years I have checked on a lot of people—a thousand, two thousand—but always after something specific, anything from an alibi to a motive for murder. With Susan Brooke I was simply checking. Because I am interested in me, I would give two bits to know which I would have preferred, to dig up something that would brand her good, or to find nothing at all worth mentioning. At the time I was just doing a job, and enjoying it carefree because there was nothing at stake for Wolfe or me.

I spent three days, parts of them, and three evenings at it. It didn't take long to cross off the Parthenon Press lead. She hadn't done her reading at the office, and only three people, two editors and a stenographer, had known her. One of the editors hadn't liked her, but I gathered, from a remark by the stenographer, that he had made a pass at her and missed.

The UN lead took longer; it took half a day to find out where she had worked. It would take another half a day for me to write, and you half an hour to read, all the items I collected. According to one source, she had got tight at a farewell luncheon for some Greek. According to another source, she hadn't. She had been so friendly with a Polish girl that she actually took her to the country for a summer weekend. Three times, or maybe four or five, she had been taken to lunch in the delegates' dining room by a Frenchman with a reputation. I followed that one up a little, but it fizzled out. She had once been seen leaving the building with a Moroccan girl, a Hungarian, and a Swede. And so forth and so on. It was very educational. The UN is wonderful for broadening a man's outlook. For instance, Turkish girls have short legs and Indian girls have flat feet.

At ten o'clock Saturday evening I mounted the stoop of the old brownstone, used my key to get in, put my coat and hat on the rack, and went down the hall to the office. Wolfe was behind his desk in the only chair in the world that really suits him, with a book, *William Shakespeare*, by A. L. Rowse. I stood while he finished a paragraph. He looked up.

I spoke. "You know, I don't think I have ever known you to take so long with a book."

He put it down. "I'm reviewing his dating of *Cymbeline*. I think he's wrong."

"Then let's send it back." I spun my chair around and sat. "I took a Moroccan girl to dinner at Rusterman's. On me. She doesn't dance, so I took her home. Today was merely more of the same, not worth reporting. Tomorrow is Sunday. I don't mind this caper, I'm enjoying it, but it's a washout. I suggest that you tell Whipple that if there's something wrong with Miss Brooke it's buried deep."

He grunted. "You like her."

"Not especially. I told you Wednesday evening that my guess was that she is comparatively clean. It still is."

"How candid are you?"

"So-so. I'm trying."

"Where is Racine?"

"Between Chicago and Milwaukee. On the lake."

He pushed his chair back, raised his bulk, walked over to the globe, which was twice as big around as he was, whirled it, and found Wisconsin.

He turned. "It's closer to Milwaukee. Is there an airplane to Milwaukee?"

"Sure." I stared. "The fare would be around eighty bucks, and then thirty bucks a day. Or more. Whipple might object."

"He will have no occasion." He returned to his chair and sat. "Veblen called it instinct of workmanship. Mine was committed when I engaged to serve Mr. Whipple. In your conversation with Miss Rowan and Miss Brooke, which you reported Wednesday evening verbatim, did you note nothing suggestive? Surely not."

"You could call it suggestive. After she said she got good and bored in Racine she said, 'Then something happened, and—' And she cut. Okay, suggestive. Maybe the roof in the big house started to leak."

"Pfui. What if Miss Brooke's past were a vital element in an investigation of great moment?"

"I would probably be in Racine now."

"Then you will go. Tomorrow. Confound it, I'm committed."

I shook my head. "Objection. Tomorrow's Sunday and I have a personal commitment."

He settled for Monday, and for Chicago instead of Milwaukee because there were more planes.

It was three above zero at twenty minutes past five Monday

afternoon when I parked the car, which I had rented in Chicago, in a lot a block away from the office of the Racine *Globe* and two blocks from the hotel where I had a reservation. I have not left the parking to the hotel since the day, a few years back, when I lost an important contact because it took them nearly half an hour to bring the car. I walked the two blocks with my bag, checked in, and went out again.

I had no appointment at the *Globe*, but Lon Cohen of the New York *Gazette* had made a phone call for me Sunday evening, and a man named James E. Leamis, the managing editor, knew I was coming. After two waits, one downstairs and one on the third floor, I was taken to him in a room that had his name on the door. He left his chair to shake hands, took my coat and hat and put them on a couch, and said it was a pleasure to meet a New York newspaperman. We sat and exchanged some remarks, and I explained that I wasn't a newspaperman; I was a private investigator doing a job for the *Gazette*. I said I supposed that Mr. Cohen had told him that the *Gazette* was thinking of running a series on the Rights of Citizens Committee, and he said no, he had told him only that I would come to ask for some information.

"But you know what the Rights of Citizens Committee is."

"Of course. There are branches in Chicago and Milwaukee, but none in Racine. Why do you come here?"

"I'm checking on a certain individual. The series will focus on the people at the New York headquarters, and one of the important ones is a young woman named Susan Brooke. I understand she's from Racine. Isn't she?"

"Yes. My God, the *Gazette* sent you out here just to check on Susan Brooke? Why?"

"No special reason. They want to fill in the background, that's all. Do you know her? Or did you?"

"I can't say I knew her. Say I was acquainted with her. I knew her brother Kenneth fairly well. Of course she's another generation. I'm twice her age."

He looked it, with his hair losing color and getting thin, and his wrinkles. He was in his shirt sleeves, with a vest, unbuttoned. I asked, "How was she regarded in Racine?"

"Well . . . all right. One of my daughters was in her class at high school. Then she went away to college—if I knew which one, I've forgotten—"

"Radcliffe."

"Oh. So actually her only background in Racine was her childhood. Her father had Racine background, and how. He was the smartest real-estate operator in southern Wisconsin. He owned this building. The family still does. I'm afraid I can't help you much, Mr. Goodwin. If what you want is dirt, I know I can't."

I had intended to ask him if anything newsworthy had happened to Susan Brooke, or about her, in the summer or fall of 1959, but I didn't. She was the *Globe's* landlady, and they might be behind on the rent. So I told him I wasn't after dirt specifically, just the picture, whatever it was. He started asking questions about the ROCC and what people in New York thought about Rockefeller and Goldwater, and I answered them to be polite.

It was dark when I emerged to the sidewalk, and the wind would freeze anything that was bare. I went back to the hotel and up to my room, where I was expecting company at six-thirty. In Chicago I had called on a man who had traded professional errands with Wolfe now and then. According to him, there was only one in Racine that was any good, by name Otto Drucker, and he had phoned him and made an appointment for me. In my nice warm room I took off my shoes and stretched out on the bed, but soon got up again. After only two blocks of that zero wind I would have been asleep in three minutes.

He was punctual, only five minutes late. As I shook hands with him at the door I didn't let my surprise show. I would never have picked him for an operative; he would have looked right at home at the desk of an assistant vice-president of a bank, with his neat well-arranged face and his friendly careful eyes. When I turned from putting his coat and hat on the bed, he asked in a friendly careful voice, "And how is Mr. Nero Wolfe?"

He was almost certainly a distinguished citizen. It had never occurred to me that a private detective could get away with it. Not Nero Wolfe. He's a citizen, and he's distinguished, but a distinguished citizen, no.

It was a very pleasant evening. He liked the idea of eating in the room. When I said I would phone room service for a menu, he said it wasn't necessary because the only things they knew how to cook were roast beef, hashed brown potatoes, and apple pie. If I reported the whole evening for you, you wouldn't enjoy it as much as I did, because mostly we talked shop. Take tailing. He knew all the tricks I had ever heard of, and, because he had been working in Racine for twenty years and everybody knew him, he had had to invent some twists that even Saul Panzer would be glad to use.

But of course the point was Susan Brooke. I didn't mention her until after we had got acquainted and had finished with the meal, which was okay, and the dishes had been taken away. All I told him was that a client was considering taking her as a partner in an important project, that anything he could tell me about her would be strictly confidential, and that he would not be quoted. I would have been disappointed in him if he hadn't asked who the client was. He did. He would have been disappointed in me if I had told him. I didn't.

He took his pipe from his mouth and tilted his head back to look at the ceiling. "Memories," he said. He plumbed his head. "I did some jobs for Susan Brooke's father. Quite a few. I could give you a line on him, but he's dead. She was just one of the kids around town, even if her name was Brooke, and as far as I know she was never in any trouble worth mentioning. I suppose you know she went away to college."

"Yeah, I know."

"And then New York. The years she was at college she wasn't here much even in the summers; she and her mother took trips. In the last eight or nine years I don't think Susan Brooke has been in Racine more than four or five months altogether. The past four years she hasn't been here at all."

"Then I'm wasting the client's money. But I understand she came here, came home, when she finished college. In nineteen fifty-nine. But maybe you wouldn't know; her father was dead then. Not long after that they left for New York. Do you happen to know how long after?"

He pulled on his pipe, found it was out, and lit it. Through the smoke screen he said, "I don't know why you're trying to sneak up on me like this. If you want to ask me about that man that killed himself, go ahead and ask, but I don't know much."

I usually manage my face fairly well, but with him there was no reason to be on guard, and it showed. What showed was how that "man that killed himself" hit me. Here, all of a sudden, was dirt. It might even be the blackest dirt, such as that she had killed a man and got it passed off as suicide. The way it hit me, it was obvious that not only had I not expected to find anything much, I hadn't wanted to.

Drucker asked, "What's the matter? Did you think I wouldn't know I was being played?"

I produced a grin. "You don't. Even if I wanted to try playing you, for practice, I know damn well I couldn't. I know nothing about the man that killed himself. I was merely checking on Susan Brooke in Racine. Maybe you're playing me?"

"No. As soon as you mentioned Susan Brooke, naturally I supposed that was the item you were checking on."

"It wasn't. I knew nothing about it. You said go ahead and ask. Okay, I ask."

"Well." He pulled at the pipe. "It was that summer when she was back from college. A young man came to town to see her, and he was seeing her, or trying to. At twenty minutes to six in the afternoon of Friday, August fourteenth, nineteen fifty-nine, he came out of the house, the Brooke house, stood on the porch, pulled a gun from his pocket, a Marley thirty-eight, and shot himself in the temple. You say you didn't know about it?"

"Yes. I did not. Was there any doubt about it?"

"None at all. Three people saw it happen. Two women on the sidewalk in front of the house and a man across the street. You would like to know about Susan Brooke, where did she fit in, but I can't tell you of my own knowledge. I only know what was printed and what a friend of mine told me who was in a position to know. The man was a college boy, Harvard. He had been pestering her to marry him, and he came to Racine to pester her some more, and she and her mother gave him the boot, so he checked out. As you know, that happens, though personally it is beyond what I can understand. There may be good and sufficient reasons for a man to kill himself, but I will never see that one of them is a woman saying no. Of course it's a form of disease. You're not married."

"No. Are you?"

"I was. She left me. It hurt my pride, but I've slept better ever since. Another thing, if a man and wife are together the way they should be, it's natural and healthy for them to talk about his work, and a private detective can't do that. Can he?"

We started talking shop and kept at it for more than an hour. I didn't try to get him back on Susan Brooke. But when he left, around ten o'clock, I told myself that the *Globe* was a morning paper, so the staff would be there now, and if her past was a vital element in an investigation of great moment, I would go and take a look. So I used the phone, got Leamis, and received permission to inspect the back file.

The wind had eased up some, but the cold hadn't, and it pinched my nose. In the *Globe* building the presses had started; there was vibration on the ground floor, and even more on the second, where I was taken to a dim and dusty room and turned over to an old geezer with no teeth, or anyway not enough. He warned me to do no clipping or tearing and led me to a bank of shelves marked 1959.

The light was bad, but I have good eyes. I started at August 7, a week before the date Drucker had named, to see if there was any mention of a Harvard man's arrival or presence in town, but there wasn't. On the fifteenth, there it was, front page. His name was Richard Ault and his home town was Evansville, Indiana. It was front page again on Sunday the sixteenth, but on Monday it was inside and on Tuesday there was nothing. I went on and finished the week but drew blanks, then went back to the first three days and read them again.

There was no hint anywhere of any covering up. The three eyewitnesses had been interviewed, and there were no discrepancies or contradictions. The porch was in plain view from the sidewalk; the two women had seen him with the gun in his hand before he had raised it, and one of them had yelled at him. The man had run across the street and had got to the porch as Mrs. Brooke and Susan emerged from the house. Susan had refused to be interviewed that evening, but had told her story to a reporter Saturday morning and had answered his questions freely.

Even if I had been hell-bent on getting something on her I would have had to cross that off and look elsewhere. I put the papers back where they belonged, told the guardian I had done no clipping or tearing, returned to the hotel, treated myself to a glass of milk in the coffee shop, and went up to bed.

I don't know whether I would have looked any further in Racine or not if there had been no interruption. Probably not, since I had learned what was in her mind when she said "then something happened," and that was what had sent me. The interruption woke me up Tuesday morning. I had left a call for eight o'clock, and when the phone rang I didn't believe it and looked at my watch. Ten after seven. I thought, Damn hotels anyway, reached for the phone, and was told I was being called from New York. I said here I am, and was figuring that in New York it was ten after eight, when Wolfe's voice came.

"Archie?"

"Right. Good morning."

"It isn't. Where are you?"

"In bed."

"I do not apologize for disturbing you. Get up and come home. Miss Brooke is dead. Her body was found last evening with the skull battered. She was murdered. Come home."

I swallowed with nothing to swallow. I started, "Where was—" and stopped. I swallowed again. "I'll leave—"

"When will you get here?"

"How do I know? Noon, one o'clock."

"Very well." He hung up.

I permitted myself to sit on the edge of the bed for ten seconds. Then I got erect, dressed, packed the bag, took the elevator down and checked out, walked to the parking lot and got the car, and headed for Chicago. I would get breakfast at the airport.

4

It wasn't noon, and it wasn't one o'clock, when I used my key on the door of the old brownstone on West 35th Street. It was five minutes to two. The plane had floated around above a fog bank for half an hour before landing at Idlewild—I mean Kennedy International Airport. I put my bag down and was taking my coat off when Fritz appeared at the end of the hall, from the kitchen, and came.

"*Grâce à Dieu*," he said. "He called the airport. You know how he is about machines. I've kept it hot. Shad roe *fines herbes*, no parsley."

"I can use it. But I—"

A roar came. "Archie!"

I went to the open door to the dining room, which is across the hall from the office. At the table, Wolfe was putting cheese on a wafer. "Nice day," I said. "You don't want to smell the herbs again so I'll eat in the kitchen with the *Times*. The one on the plane was the early edition."

We get two copies of the *Times*, one for Wolfe, who has a tray breakfast in his room, and one for me. I proceeded to the kitchen, and there was my *Times*, propped on the rack, on the little table where I always eat breakfast. Even when I'm away for a week on some errand Fritz probably puts it there every morning. He would. I sat and got it and looked for the headline, but in a moment was interrupted by Fritz with the platter and a hot plate. I helped myself and took a bite of the roe and a piece of crusty roll dabbed in the sauce, which is one of Fritz's best when he leaves the parsley out.

The details were about as scanty as in the early edition. Susan Brooke's corpse had been found shortly before nine o'cock Monday evening in a room on the third floor of a building on 128th Street, a walk-up of course, by a man named Dunbar Whipple, who was on the staff of the Rights of Citizens Committee. Her skull had been crushed by repeated blows. I already knew that much. Also I already knew what the late city edition added: that Susan Brooke had been a volunteer worker for the ROCC, and she had lived with her widowed mother in a Park Avenue apartment; and that Dunbar Whipple was twenty-three years old and was the son of Paul Whipple, an assistant professor of anthropology at Columbia University. One thing I had not actually known but could have guessed if I had put my mind on it: the police and the district attorney's office had started an investigation.

When the roe and sauce and rolls were where they belonged, and some salad, I refilled my coffee cup and took it to the office. Wolfe was at his desk, tapping his nose with a pencil, scowling at a crossword puzzle. I went to my desk, sat, and sipped coffee. After a while he switched the scowl to me, realized I hadn't earned it, and erased it.

"Confound it," he said, "it's preposterous and insulting that I might lose your services and talents merely through the whim of a mechanism. How high up were you at noon?"

"Oh, four miles. I know. You regard anything and everything beyond your control as an insult. You—"

"No. Not in nature. Only in what men contrive."

I nodded. "And what they do. For instance, committing murder. Have you any news besides what's in the *Times?*"

"No."

"Any callers? Whipple?"

"No."

"Do you want a report on Racine?"

"No. To what purpose?"

"I merely ask. I need a shave. Since there's nothing urgent, apparently, I'll go up and use a mechanism. If I did report I wouldn't have to speak ill of the dead." I left the chair. "At least I won't—"

The doorbell rang. I went to the hall for a look through the one-way glass, saw two men on the stoop, and stepped back in. "Two Whipples, father and son. I have never seen the son, but of course it is. Have they an appointment?"

He glared. I stood, but evidently he thought the glare needed no help, so I went down the hall to the front and opened the door. Paul Whipple said, "We have to see Mr. Wolfe. This is my son Dunbar."

"He's expecting you," I said, which was probably true, and sidestepped to give them room.

A day or two earlier I would have been glad to meet the Negro specimen that Susan Brooke intended to marry, just to size him up. All right, I was meeting him, and he looked like

Sugar Ray Robinson after a hard ten rounds, except that he was a little darker. A day or two earlier he would probably have been handsome and jaunty; now he was a wreck. So was his father. When I started a hand for his hat he let go before I reached it, and it dropped to the floor.

In the office I nodded the father to the red leather chair and moved up one of the yellow ones for the son. Dunbar sat, but Whipple stood and looked at Wolfe, bleary-eyed. Wolfe spoke. "Sit down, Mr. Whipple. You're crushed. Have you eaten?"

That wasn't flip. Wolfe is convinced that when real trouble comes the first thing to do is eat.

Dunbar blurted at Wolfe, "What did you do? What did you do?"

Whipple shook his head at him. "Take it easy, son." He twisted around to look at the chair, saw it was there, and sat. He looked at Wolfe. "You know what happened."

Wolfe nodded. "I have read the paper. Mr. Whipple. Many people in distress have sat in that chair. Sometimes I cannot supply advice or services, but I can always supply food. I doubt if you have eaten. Have you?"

"We're not here to eat!" Dunbar blurted. "What did you do?"

"I'll talk, son," Whipple told him. To Wolfe: "I know what you mean. I made him eat a little just now, on the way here. I felt I had to tell him what I asked you to do, and he wants to know what you did. You understand that he's—uh—overwrought. As you said, in distress. Of course I would like to know too, what you did. You understand that."

"Yes. I myself have done nothing." Wolfe leaned back, drew in air through his nose, all there was room for, which was plenty, and let it out through his mouth. "Archie. Tell them."

Dunbar blurted at me, "You're Archie Goodwin."

"Right." I moved my eyes to Whipple. "Did you tell him exactly what you asked Mr. Wolfe to do?"

"Yes. Exactly."

"Okay. A friend of mine named Lily Rowan invited Miss Brooke to lunch, and I was there. At lunch nothing was discussed but the ROCC. After lunch Miss Rowan gave Miss Brooke a check for a thousand dollars for the ROCC and asked her some questions about herself. Nothing cheeky, just the usual line. Miss Brooke mentioned that she had worked for the Parthenon Press and at the UN, and I spent three days checking that, mostly at the UN. I found nothing that you could use, and yesterday I took a plane to Chicago and drove to Racine, Wisconsin. At Racine I talked with two men who had known Miss Brooke and her family, a newspaperman and a private detective, and got no hint of anything you could use. You wanted to find out what was wrong with her. Correct?"

"Yes."

"I decided that there was nothing worth mentioning wrong with her and never had been. When I turned in at the hotel last night I intended to leave this morning, and at seven a.m. Mr. Wolfe phoned and told me what had happened, and I left right away and returned to New York. Any questions?"

Dunbar moved. On his feet, peering down at me, his shoulders hunched, he looked like Sugar Ray starting the tenth round, not ending it. "You're lying," he said, not blurting. "You're covering up, I don't know what, but I'm going to. You know who killed her." He wheeled to Wolfe. "So do you, you fat ape."

"Sit down," Wolfe said.

Dunbar put his fists on Wolfe's desk and leaned over at him. "And you're going to tell me," he said through his teeth.

Wolfe shook his head. "You're driveling, Mr. Whipple. I

don't know what you're like when you are in command of your
faculties, but I know what you're like now. You're an ass.
Neither Mr. Goodwin nor I had ever heard of you or Miss
Brooke. I don't suppose you suspect your father of hiring me to
arrange for her death, and I doubt if—"

"That's not—"

"I'm talking. I doubt if even in your present condition you
suspect Mr. Goodwin or me of doing it unbidden. But you
may—"

"I didn't—"

"I'm talking! You may understandably surmise that in his
contacts with various persons Mr. Goodwin unwittingly said or
did something which led to a situation that resulted in the
death of Miss Brooke. You may even surmise that he was aware
of it, or is. In that case, I suggest that you sit down and ask him,
civilly. He is fairly headstrong and can't be bullied. I stopped
trying years ago. As for me, I know nothing. Mr. Goodwin's
plane was late, he arrived only an hour ago, and we haven't
discussed it."

Dunbar backed away, came in contact with the rim of the
chair seat, bent his knees, and sat. His head went down and
his hands came up to cover his face.

Whipple said, "Take it easy, son."

I cleared my throat. "I have had a lot of practice reporting
conversations verbatim. Also tones and looks and reactions. I
am better at it than anyone around except a man named Saul
Panzer. I don't believe that anything I have said or done had
anything to do with the death of Susan Brooke, but if Mr.
Wolfe tells me to—I was and am working for him—I'll be glad
to report it in full. I think it would be a waste of time. As for
my covering up, nuts."

Whipple's jaw was working. "I hope you're right, Mr. Goodwin. God knows I do. If I was responsible—" He couldn't finish it.

Dunbar's head came up, his face to me. "I'll apologize."

"You don't have to. Skip it."

"But maybe you'll tell me who you saw and what was said. Later. I know I'm not in command of my faculties, I haven't got any faculties. I've had no sleep and I don't want to sleep. I answered questions all night and all morning. They think I killed her. By God, they think *I* killed her!"

I nodded. "But you didn't?"

He stared. His eyes were in no condition for staring. "My God, do you think I did?"

"I don't think. I don't know you. I don't know anything."

"I know him," the father said. He was looking at Wolfe. "He wanted to come here because he thought . . . what he said. I didn't know what to think, but I was afraid. I was mortally afraid that I was responsible. Now perhaps I wasn't; I can hope I wasn't. And I wanted to come for another reason. They are going to arrest him. They think he killed her. They are going to charge him with murder. We need your help."

Wolfe tightened his lips.

Whipple went on. "I came and asked your help when I shouldn't have. That was wrong, and I bitterly regret it. I thought at the time I was justified, but I wasn't. I hated to tell my son about it, but I had to. He had to know. Now I *must* ask your help. Now it would be right for me to remind you of that speech. 'But if you shield him because he is your color there is a great deal to say. You are rendering your race a serious disservice. You are helping to perpetuate—'"

"That's enough," Wolfe snapped. "It isn't pertinent. It has no bearing on the present situation."

"Not directly. But you persuaded me to help you by prescribing adherence to the agreements of human society. I was an ignorant boy, immature, and you tricked me—I don't complain, it was a legitimate trick. I don't say this is analogous, but you had a problem and asked me to help, and I have one and I'm asking you to help. My son is going to be charged with murder."

Wolfe's eyes were narrowed at him. "They have questioned him for hours and aren't holding him."

"They will. When they're ready."

"Then he will need a lawyer."

"He'll need more than a lawyer. The way it looks. He'll need you."

"You may be exaggerating his jeopardy." Wolfe went to Dunbar. "Are you under control, Mr. Whipple?"

"No, I'm not," he said.

"I'll try you anyway. You said they think you killed her. Is that merely your fancy or has it a basis?"

"They think it has a basis, but it hasn't."

"That begs the question. I'll try again. Why do they think it has a basis?"

"Because I was there. Because she and I—we were friends. Because she was white and I'm black. Because of the billy, the club that killed her."

Wolfe grunted. "You'll have to elucidate. First the club. Was it yours?"

"I had it. It's a club that had been used by a policeman in a town in Alabama to beat up two colored boys. I got it—it doesn't matter how I got it, I had it. I had had it on my desk at the office for several months."

"Was it on your desk yesterday?"

"No. Susan—" He stopped.

"Yes?"

Dunbar looked at his father and back at Wolfe. "I don't know why I stopped. I've told all this to the police, I knew I had to, because it was known. Miss Brooke had rented and furnished a little apartment on One Hundred and Twenty-eighth Street, and the club was there. She had taken it there."

"When?"

"About a month ago."

"Have the police found your fingerprints on it?"

"I don't know, but I don't think so. I think it had been wiped."

"Why do you think it had been wiped?"

"Because they didn't say definitely that it had my fingerprints on it."

Fair enough. Apparently he had got control. Answering questions will often do that.

"A reasonable assumption," Wolfe conceded. "So much for the means. As for the opportunity, you were there, but there is the question of your prior movements yesterday, say from noon on. Of course the police went into that thoroughly. Tell me briefly. I am examining the official assumption that you killed her."

Dunbar was sitting straighter. "At noon I was at my desk in the office. At a quarter to one I met two men at a restaurant for lunch. I was back at the office a little before three. At four o'clock I went to a conference in the office of Mr. Henchy, the executive director. It ended a little after six, and when I went to my room there was a message on my desk. Miss Brooke and I had arranged to meet at the apartment at eight o'clock, and the message was that she had phoned that she couldn't get there until nine or a little later. That was convenient for me because I had a dinner engagement with one of the men who had been at the conference. It was twenty-five minutes past eight when we parted at the subway entrance on Forty-second Street, and it was five minutes past nine when I got to One Hundred and Twenty-eighth Street and entered."

"And discovered the body."

"Yes."

Wolfe glanced up at the clock. "Will it jar you to tell me what you did?"

"No. She was there on the floor. There was blood, and I got some on my hands and my sleeve. For a while, I don't know how long, I didn't do anything. The club was there on a chair. I didn't touch it. There was no use getting a doctor. I sat on the bed and tried to think, to decide what to do. I suppose you think that wasn't natural, with her there dead on the floor, for me to be worrying about *me*. Maybe it wasn't, but that's what I did. You wouldn't ever understand because you're white."

"Pfui. You're a man, and so am I."

"That's what you say. Words. I knew I had to face it or do something with—with *it*. I would have, too, but I just barely had sense enough to know I wouldn't get away with it. It couldn't be done. I went and looked in the phone book for the number of police headquarters and dialed it. That was at twenty minutes to ten. I had been there over half an hour."

"The delay was ill-advised but explicable. You have come to grief, certainly, but a murder charge? What will they do for motive?"

Dunbar stared. "You don't mean that. A Negro and a white girl?"

"Nonsense. New York isn't Utopia, but neither is it Dixie."

"That's right. In Dixie I wouldn't be sitting in a fine big room telling a famous detective about it. Here in New York they're more careful about it; they take their time. But about motive, with a Negro they take motive for granted. He's a shine, he's a mistake, he was born with motives white men don't have. It may be nonsense, but it's the way it is."

"With the scum, yes. With dolts and idiots."

"With everybody. Lots of them don't know it. Most of them up here wouldn't say that word, nigger, but they've got that word in them. *Everybody.* It's in them buried somewhere, but it's not dead. Some of them don't know they've got it and they wouldn't believe it, but it's there. That's what I knew I'd have to face when I sat there on the bed last night and tried to decide what to do."

"And you made the right decision. Disposing of the body, however ingeniously, would have been fatal." Wolfe shook his head. "As for your comments about that word, nigger, its special significance for you distorts your understanding. Consider the words that are buried in *you* but not dead. Consider even the ones that are not buried, that you use: for instance, 'fat ape.' May I assume that a man who resembles an ape, or one who is fat, or both, could not expect just treatment or consideration from you? Certainly not. The mind or soul or psyche —take the term you prefer—of any man below the level of consciousness is a preposterous mishmash of cesspool and garden. Heaven only knows what I have in mine as synonyms for 'woman'; I'm glad I don't know."

He turned to the father. "Mr. Whipple. The best service I could render you, and your son, would be to feed you. Say an omelet with mushrooms and watercress. Twenty minutes. Do you like watercress?"

Whipple blinked his bleary eyes. "Then you're not going to help us."

"There's nothing I can do. I can't fend the blow; it has landed. Your assumption that your son will be charged with murder is probably illusory. You're distraught."

Whipple's mouth twitched. "Mushrooms and watercress. No, thank you." His hand went inside his jacket and came out with a checkfold. He opened it. "How much do I owe you?"

"Nothing. I owed you."

"Mr. Goodwin's trip. To Racine."

"You didn't authorize it. I sent him." Wolfe pushed his chair back and stood up. "You will excuse me. I have an appointment. I'm sorry I undertook that job; it was frivolous. And I deplore your misfortune." He headed for the door.

He was fudging. It was 3:47, and his afternoon session in the plant rooms was from four to six.

5

Fifty hours went by.

Like you and everyone else, I have various sources of information about what goes on: newspapers, magazines, radio, television, taxicab drivers, random talk here and there, friends, and enemies. I also have two special ones: Lon Cohen, confidential assistant to the publisher of the *Gazette*, and a woman who is on intimate terms, not familial, with a certain highly distinguished citizen, for whom I once did a big favor. But the news of the arrest of Dunbar Whipple came from none of those sources; it came from Inspector Cramer of Homicide South, whom I couldn't exactly call an enemy and wouldn't presume to call a friend.

During the two days I had not only read the newspapers but had also phoned Lon Cohen a couple of times to ask if there was anything hot about the Susan Brooke murder that wasn't being printed. There wasn't, unless you would call it hot that her brother Kenneth had socked an assistant district attorney on the beak, or that there was nothing to the rumor that it was being hushed up that she had been pregnant. She hadn't been. Of course a lot was being printed: that her handbag, on a table in the apartment, had had more than a hundred dollars in it; that an expensive gold pin had been on her dress and a ring with a big emerald had been on her finger (I had seen the ring); that she had bought a bottle of wine at a package store, and several items at a delicatessen, shortly before eight o'clock; that her mother was prostrated and inaccessible; that everyone at the ROCC had been or was being questioned; and so on. The *News* came out ahead on shots of Susan Brooke, with one in a bikini on a Puerto Rico beach, but the *Gazette* had the best one of Dunbar Whipple. Handsome and jaunty.

I wasn't surprised when, at 6:05 Thursday afternoon, Inspector Cramer showed. I had been expecting him or Sergeant Purley Stebbins, or at least a phone call, since Wednesday noon, when Lily Rowan had phoned to tell me she had had an official caller. Of course they had done a routine check on Susan Brooke's recent activities, of course someone at the ROCC had told them about her lunch with Miss Lily Rowan and Lily's contribution to the cause, of course they had called on Miss Rowan, and of course Lily had told the caller about me, since someone else would—for instance, the hallman—if she didn't. So I had been expecting company, and when the doorbell rang and I saw Cramer's burly figure and round red face and battered old felt hat on the stoop, I went and opened up and said, peeved, "You took your time. We've been expecting you for days."

He spoke to me as he entered. Sometimes he doesn't; he just tramps down the hall. The fact that he spoke, and even thanked me for taking his hat and coat, showed that he had come not to claim but to ask. When he entered the office, naturally he didn't offer a hand, since he knows that Wolfe is not a shaker, but before he lowered his fanny onto the red leather chair he uttered a polite greeting and actually made a try at being sociable by asking, "And how are the orchids?"

Wolfe's brows went up. "Passable, thank you. A pot of Miltonia roezli has fourteen scapes."

"Is that so." Cramer sat and pulled his feet in. "Busy? Am I interrupting something?"

"No, sir."

"No case and no client?"

"Yes. None."

"I thought possibly you were on a job for Dunbar Whipple. I thought possibly he hired you when he was here Tuesday with his father."

"No. It didn't seem to me that he was sufficiently menaced to require my services."

Cramer nodded. "That's possible. It's also possible that it seemed to you he was a murderer, so you bowed out. I say 'bowed out' because you did have a client. His father."

"Did I?"

"Sure. We know all about that, including Goodwin's trip to Racine. Since you're out of it, I might as well be frank. He's at the district attorney's office and when he leaves he'll be taken to a cell. He'll be formally charged in the morning. I'll—"

"Murder?"

"Yes. I'll frankly admit that if you had told me you had taken him on I would have expected answers to a lot of questions, and Goodwin would have been wanted downtown. Now he may not have to go." He turned to me. "In your check on Su-

san Brooke, what did you find out about her relations with
Dunbar Whipple?"

I looked at Wolfe. He shook his head and looked at Cramer.
"If you please. Is the decision definite to hold Dunbar Whipple
without bail on a murder charge?"

"Yes. That's why I'm here."

"Has he a lawyer?"

"Yes. He's at the district attorney's office now."

"His name, please?"

"Why?"

Wolfe turned a palm up. "Must I get it from the morning
paper?"

Cramer turned both palms up. "Harold R. Oster. A Negro.
Counsel for the Rights of Citizens Committee."

Wolfe's eyes came to me. "Archie, get Mr. Parker."

I got the phone. I didn't have to consult the book for either
of the numbers, office or home, of Nathaniel Parker, the member of the bar. Knowing he was often at his office after hours
I tried that one first and got him. Wolfe took his phone, and I
stayed on.

"Mr. Parker? I need some information confidentially. You will
not be quoted. Do you know a lawyer named Harold R. Oster?"

"I know of him. I've met him. He's with the Rights of Citizens Committee. He handles civil rights cases."

"Yes. How efficient would he be as counsel for a man charged
with murder?"

"Oh." Pause. "Dunbar Whipple?"

"Yes."

"Are you on *that*?"

"I merely want information."

"You usually do. Well . . . confidentially, I would say no.

He has ability, no doubt of that, but in my opinion he might take a wrong line in a case where—a Negro killing a white woman. I mean *charged* with killing her. If I were Dunbar Whipple, I would want a different kind of man. Of course I may be completely wrong, but—"

"Enough, Mr. Parker, wrong or not. Thank you. You won't be quoted." Wolfe hung up and turned. "Archie. Did Dunbar Whipple kill Susan Brooke?"

I know him so well. Anyone might suppose he was showing off to Cramer, showing him how eccentric and unique he was, but no. He merely wanted to know what I would say. If we had been alone I would have told him that one would get him ten that Dunbar was innocent, but with Cramer there I preferred to skip the odds.

"No," I said.

He nodded. "Get Mr. Whipple."

Before turning to the phone I shot a glance at Cramer. Chin down, eyes narrowed, and lips tight, he was glued to Wolfe. He knows him fairly well too, and he suspected what was coming.

It would have cramped Wolfe's style a little if Whipple hadn't been at home, but he was. He answered the phone. I started to tell him that Mr. Wolfe wanted to speak to him, but Wolfe was at his phone and cut in.

"This is Nero Wolfe, Mr. Whipple. Can you hear me?"

"Yes."

"I owe you an apology. You were right, and I was wrong. I have just learned that your son is being held on a charge of murder. I am convinced that the charge is unfounded. If you want my services on your son's behalf, I offer them without fee. My previous undertaking to discharge my obligation to you was fatuous; I should have said no. Now I say yes."

Silence. Then: "His lawyer phoned an hour ago that he would probably be home by eight o'clock."

"His lawyer was wrong. I have more accurate information. Do you accept my offer?"

"Yes. Of course. We'll pay all we can."

"You'll pay nothing. My self-esteem needs repairs. But there's a question: the approval of your son and his lawyer."

"They'll approve. I know they will. But how did you learn—are you sure . . ."

"Yes. A policeman is sitting here in the chair you sat in. When you have the approval of your son and his lawyer, let me know and I'll proceed. I must talk with you and the lawyer."

"Of course. I knew this—I knew it would happen, but now that—now that—"

"Yes. Some time has been lost. Let me know." He hung up and swiveled.

Cramer asked, cold and slow, "What kind of a goddam play is this?"

Wolfe pinched his nose. "I believe I have never told you of an experience I had years ago at a place in West Virginia. I wanted to leave and come home, and I wanted a certain favor from a certain man. A young colored man made it possible for me to realize both desires. His name was Paul Whipple. I hadn't seen him since until ten days ago—no, eleven. Now I'll even the score."

"The hell you will. You can't possibly know that Dunbar Whipple didn't kill that girl. The only way you could know that would be if you thought you knew who did kill her."

"I haven't the slightest idea who killed her."

"I don't believe you. It's obvious that when Goodwin was checking on her he dug up something that you intend to use to pull one of your goddam fancy stunts. You're not going to. I told you that if you had taken him on Goodwin would have been wanted downtown, and now I'm telling you that I'm taking you too. To the district attorney." He rose. "If you want it done right, you're under arrest as material witnesses. Come on."

Wolfe, in no hurry, put his hands on the desk rim to push his chair back, arose, and got the edge of his vest between thumbs and forefingers to pull it down. "We shall of course stand mute and get bail tomorrow. May we have two minutes to call Mr. Parker? Get him, Archie."

I slanted my eyes up at Cramer, waiting politely for permission, since I was under arrest. He stood and breathed for ten seconds. He spoke. "You told Whipple that the charge against his son is unfounded. Let's hear you reply to what I said, that if you say Dunbar Whipple didn't kill her you think you know who did."

"I did reply. I have no idea who killed her."

"Then why didn't he?"

"I am not obliged to account for a conclusion I have formed. But I tell you on my word of honor—a phrase I respect, as you know—that the conclusion has no evidential basis. I know nothing of the circumstances that led to the death of Susan Brooke that you don't know; indeed, I know much less than you do. I offer a suggestion. I am now committed to act in the interest of Mr. Whipple, I would like to proceed without delay, and I would rather not spend tonight and part of tomorrow in custody, mute or not. I'm going to ask Mr. Goodwin to type a full report, with all conversations verbatim, of his investigation of Susan Brooke, and I offer to send you a copy of it, with his affidavit. That should satisfy you."

"What about you?"

"Dismiss me. All my knowledge of the matter will be contained in Mr. Goodwin's report. Still my word of honor."

"When will I get the report?"

"I can't say. How long will it take, Archie?"

"It depends," I told him. "If you want it all, every word, say forty hours. Three days and evenings. I talked with many people about many things. If you want only what could possibly be relevant, ten or twelve hours should do it. The affidavit could cover it."

"Tomorrow afternoon," Cramer said. "By five o'clock."

"Maybe, but no guarantee."

He regarded Wolfe, opened his mouth and closed it again, about-faced, and was going. Wolfe raised his voice to tell his back, "We are under arrest!"

"Balls," Cramer said without stopping. As I got up and went to the hall to see that he was outside when the door shut, I was thinking that you couldn't blame him for being rude. He was facing the fact that they were slapping the big one on a man that Nero Wolfe had decided to take on. I didn't offer to help him with his hat and coat; it wouldn't have been appreciated. When he was out and the door shut I stepped back in the office. Wolfe was back in his chair, looking sour.

I went to my desk and sat. "At least twelve hours," I said. "I might as well be in jail." I swiveled, got out paper and carbons, and swung the typewriter around.

"What are you doing?" he demanded.

"Starting that damn report."

"Why don't you badger me first?"

"Waste of time. Anyway, didn't I say no?"

"Yes. Why?"

I swiveled to face him. "You know why, since you phoned Whipple. When he barked at you, 'What did you do, what did you do,' I thought to myself, so he didn't kill her. If he had killed her of course he would be putting on an act, but that act was just too good. Only a genius could be that good, and I've never seen any genius besides you. Then when he told me I knew who killed her. Then when he apologized to you. Do I have to go on?"

"No. It was manifest. He couldn't possibly have been dissembling. You're aware that the report is required not only for Mr. Cramer. I must have it."

"Sure. Proceeding as usual. Giving me a long, mean, extremely difficult job."

I turned and got at the paper and carbons.

6

It took eleven hours plus, four hours Thursday evening and
most of Friday. Thirty-two pages and the affidavit. That may
seem slow, but for most of it I had no notes. At a quarter past
four Friday afternoon I put it in an envelope with a label addressed to Inspector Cramer, took it to a notary public on
Eighth Avenue to have the affidavit made official, and then, in
a taxi, to Homicide South on 20th Street. I also took a taxi back.
It was a nice sunny winter day for a walk, but the *Gazette*
was on the stands and there was an item in it which I wanted
to enjoy at leisure.

There had been interruptions. Whipple had phoned late
Thursday evening to say that Oster, the lawyer, had been glad
to hear that he would have Nero Wolfe's help and had approved on behalf of his client. At eight-thirty Friday morning,
already at my desk, I was buzzed by Wolfe on the house phone
from his room and instructed to call Lon Cohen and tell him

that if he cared to send a reporter to 35th Street we would have
an item that might be printable; and furthermore I was told to
send the reporter up to the plant rooms if he came between
nine and eleven. He came a little after ten, and Fritz took
him up in the elevator. That wasn't unprecedented but it was
out of the ordinary. It was too bad I couldn't tell Dunbar Whipple that, in the interest of a Negro, Wolfe was making an exception he had rarely made in the interest of any white man. I
wondered then, and I still do, whether words had anything to
do with it, knowing how he is about words. As he had told me,
discussing words one evening at the dinner table, *negro* means
black in Spanish and *nero* means black in Italian. And he had
been born in Montenegro, Black Mountain. Maybe something buried in him but not dead, in his cesspool and/or
garden.

Of the other phone calls I need to report only one, shortly
after lunch, from Oster, when it was arranged that he and
Whipple would come at six o'clock for a conference.

In the cab returning from 20th Street I read the item three
times. It was on page 3, with the headline: NERO WOLFE SITS IN.
Not bad. About anyone else it would probably have been
STEPS IN. God knows he sits. It went:

> Nero Wolfe, the well-known private detective, is working
> on the Susan Brooke murder case. He announced today that
> he has been engaged by Harold R. Oster, attorney for Dunbar
> Whipple, who has been charged with the murder (see page
> 1), to investigate certain aspects of the affair.
> According to the record, not one of Wolfe's clients has ever
> been convicted of murder. Asked this morning by a *Gazette*
> reporter if he didn't feel that in this case he was endangering
> his record, he replied with a flat no. He said that he has good
> reason to believe that Dunbar Whipple is innocent, and he is

confident that, working with Oster, he will be able to procure evidence that will clear him.

He declined to disclose his reasons for believing that Whipple is innocent or the nature of the evidence he expects to get. But for some people the mere fact that he is willing to have it known publicly that he is engaged in the defense of Whipple will be significant. Others will say that there is always a first time.

No picture of the well-known detective, though there were a dozen shots of him in the *Gazette* morgue. I'd have to write a letter to the editor.

When I entered the old brownstone and went to the office I noticed something. The *Gazette* is delivered there every day around five o'clock, and it wasn't on my desk, and I wanted the extra copy. I went to the kitchen and asked Fritz if he had it, and he said no, Wolfe had phoned down from the plant rooms to bring it up. More out of the ordinary. He likes to see his name in the paper as well as you do, but he always waits until he comes down to the office. As I got the milk from the refrigerator and poured a glass I was thinking that if you stick around long enough you'll see everything.

Whipple and Oster arrived early. One of the many Wolfe-made rules in that house is that when a client and his lawyer are both present the client gets the red leather chair, but that time it wasn't followed. Oster shot a glance around and went straight to it. He was tall and broad, with skin the color of dark honey, the kind Wolfe prefers—I mean honey—and he moved like a man who is in charge and intends to stay in charge. I was curious to see what would happen if Wolfe tried to shift him to the yellow chair.

He didn't bother. The sound came of the elevator jolting to a stop, and he entered. The *Gazette* was in his hand. He nodded left and right and headed between them for his desk, but Oster was up with a hand out. Wolfe halted, shook his head, said distinctly, "My wrist," and went to his chair.

Oster sat down and asked, "Hurt your wrist?"

"Long ago." Wolfe looked at the client. "Have you seen your son, Mr. Whipple?"

Whipple said he had.

"And he accepts my offer?"

"*I* have accepted it," Oster said. He had the kind of deep baritone that bounces off of walls. "I'm his attorney and I make the decisions."

Wolfe ignored him. "I wish to make sure," he told Whipple, "that your son knows I am working for him and approves. Have you told him—"

"That's impertinent!" Oster cut in. "You know damn well, Wolfe, that a counselor *acts* for his client. If you don't, you're a lot more ignorant than a man like you ought to be. I'm surprised. I'm astonished, and I may have to reconsider my acceptance of your offer."

Wolfe regarded him. "Are you through, Mr. Oster?"

"I said I *may* have to reconsider."

"I mean are you through speaking?"

"I'm through with that."

"Good. I goaded you deliberately. I'm aware of the status of a counselor. What concerns me is my status. In order to do a satisfactory job for Mr. Whipple, I must begin with an assumption which you will almost certainly reject. Knowing that we would inevitably clash, I thought it well to show you at once that I am arbitrary and contumelious. If there must be a clash, let's have it and see what happens. My initial assumption is that Dunbar Whipple did not kill Susan Brooke, but that she was killed by someone who works for or with the Rights of Citizens Committee. That is—"

"You're damn right I reject it." Oster turned to Whipple. "He's impossible. Listen to him. Impossible!"

"You're a bungler," Wolfe said, not clashing, just stating a fact.

Oster goggled at him, speechless.

"Even if you repudiate my assumption," Wolfe said, "as the man responsible for Dunbar Whipple's defense you should want to know why I make it. It's tentative, merely a place to start; I must start somewhere. The most pointed known fact about the murderer is that he knew about that apartment, and that Miss Brooke was there or probably was. Since her money and jewelry were not taken, he was not a random marauder; moreover, he didn't try to pose as one by taking them. I don't suppose there were many people who knew of the apartment; apparently, from accounts and hints in the newspapers, there were very few. In an effort to find them, the most likely place should be tried first. I have a question. Dunbar Whipple is your client. If you could clear him only by exposing the real culprit, and if the culprit were someone connected with the organization of which you are the counsel, and if you had it in your power to expose him, would you do so?"

Of course he had to say yes. He added, "But that's three ifs."

"Not the first one, though I said 'if.' Come, Mr. Oster, let's be realistic. Yesterday at this hour a police inspector was sitting in that chair, and we talked at length. I believe that your client is in grave jeopardy unless we produce a substitute. Don't you?"

"Was it Cramer?"

"Yes."

"That damned Cossack."

"Not by definition." Wolfe flipped it aside. "I won't press you for an answer; your reputation for acumen is answer enough." Vinegar, then butter. "Dunbar Whipple entered that apartment shortly after nine o'clock and remained there continuously until the police arrived some forty minutes later; he says so. The only feasible method of proving that Susan Brooke died before he arrived is to produce the person who killed her. Let's find him. The ROCC is not the only place to look, certainly. Your report, Archie?"

I got it from a drawer. He asked, "You have an extra copy?"

I nodded. "I made three."

"Give it to Mr. Oster. That, sir, is a complete report, omitting nothing that could possibly be pertinent, of the investigation of Susan Brooke undertaken by me at the request of Mr. Paul Whipple. I haven't studied it yet, but I shall. I suggest that you do the same. Any hint it contains, however slight, will of course be considered. But as soon as possible I must see—"

He stopped short. He slapped the desk blotter. "Confound it. I'm a ninny. I haven't asked you: have you in mind a ready and cogent defense?"

Oster was flipping the pages of the report. He looked up. "Not . . . I wouldn't say . . . not ready, no."

"Have you any knowledge or suspicion, however vague, of the identity of the murderer?"

"No."

"Have you, Mr. Whipple?"

"No," Whipple said. "Absolutely none. But I have a question. Not just curiosity, my son wants to know, and I told him

I'd ask you. A lawyer will defend a man even if he thinks he's guilty, but you won't. You must think, you must be fairly sure, that my son is innocent. He wants to know why."

"Does it matter?"

"It does to him."

"Pfui. Tell him because he's a Negro and Susan Brooke was a white girl. That should satisfy him. To satisfy you: partly the absence of a known motive for him, but mostly what he said and did in this room Tuesday afternoon. Either it was an inspired performance or he is innocent, and I don't think he is inspired. I think he's a callow stripling. Please tell him so." Wolfe went back to Oster. "I tried baiting a hook this morning. Have you seen today's *Gazette?*"

"No."

Wolfe picked it up from his desk and stretched his arm. "Here. It's open to the page. Third column, my name in the headline."

Oster took it and read it, taking his time, and reached to hand it to Whipple. "Damn it, you're worse than arbitrary," he told Wolfe. "You know damn well you should have cleared it with me. Bait? Where's the hook?"

Wolfe nodded. "I'm merely showing you that the assumption you reject is not exclusive. As for the bait and hook, I thought it worth trying. It's barely possible that someone, satisfied and apparently secure because the police have settled on Dunbar Whipple, will be disquieted by the news that I am taking a hand and will do something. Remote, certainly."

"It certainly is. How conceited can you get? Understand this, Wolfe: you're under my direction. I'm glad to have this report; that's fine. But anything you do must first have my approval. Understand?"

Wolfe shook his head. "I don't work that way, but let it pass for the moment. For what I intend to do first I need not only your approval but your assistance. Tomorrow evening at nine o'clock I would like to see, here, the entire staff of the office of the Rights of Citizens Committee. Including Mr. Henchy, the executive director."

Oster smiled, a broad smile. "Listen, Wolfe. You began by trying to get a rise out of me, and you got it. Once is enough. Go soak your head."

"Not now. I'm using it. If you don't approve and won't help, I'll get those people here myself. I must see them."

"If you try that, you're through." Oster stood up. "In fact, you're through now. You're out." He turned to Whipple. "Come on, Paul. He's impossible. Come on."

"No," Whipple said.

"What do you mean, no? You heard him! He's impossible!"

"But he . . ." Whipple let it hang. "I think you should consider it, Harold. Isn't it reasonable, his wanting to see them and ask them questions? It isn't—"

"I have seen them and asked them questions! I know them! Come on! If we need a detective, there are others!"

"Not like him," Whipple said. "No, Harold. You're being hasty. If you don't want to ask them to come, all right, I will. I'm sure Tom Henchy will see that it's reasonable. He's a—"

"You do that, Paul, and you'll get another lawyer, you and Dunbar. I'm warning you. I'm telling you."

"You're being hasty, Harold."

"I'm telling you!"

"You certainly are." Whipple's head was tilted back. I had his profile, and for the first time I saw in him the cocky college boy at Kanawha Spa years and years back. "I know you're a good lawyer, Harold, but I don't know if you're good enough to get Dunbar out of this trouble. I'm being frank, and I doubt it. If anybody can, Nero Wolfe can. If it has to be you or Nero Wolfe, I'll see Dunbar in the morning and tell him what I think, and he'll agree. I'm sure he will." His eyes went to Wolfe. "Mr. Wolfe, it's not only the impression you made on me long ago when I was a raw kid. I've followed your career. As far as I'm concerned, you're in charge." Back to Oster: "Don't go, Harold. Sit down."

Oster was chewing his lip. "It's ridiculous," he said. "I'm an attorney-at-law, a respected member of the bar. He's a—a gumshoe."

"Mr. Oster," Wolfe said.

"What?"

"I suggest that Mr. Whipple's extravagance should be ignored. Let's put it that the legal defense of Dunbar Whipple is in your hands, and the search for evidence to support that defense is in my hands. I knew we would clash, and we have. There are no casualties. Oblige me by sitting down. Naturally I expected, and expect, you to be present at the conference tomorrow evening. If you wish to object to anything I say or do, you have a tongue. You have indeed. I don't wonder that you tried to drum me out; I'm difficult, though not really impossible. If you wish to debate it with Mr. Whipple, you can do so later." He looked at the clock. "No doubt you have information for me, and suggestions, and in less than half an hour it will be dinnertime. If you and Mr. Whipple will dine with us, we'll have the evening for it. Wild duck with Vatel sauce— wine vinegar, egg yolk, tomato paste, butter, cream, salt and pepper, shallots, tarragon, chervil, and peppercorns. Is any of those distasteful to you?"

Oster said no.

"To you, Mr. Whipple?"

Whipple said no.

"Tell Fritz, Archie."

I got up and went to the kitchen. It was a good thing neither of them had said yes, for Fritz was well along with the sauce, as Wolfe had known he would be. He didn't welcome my news. Not that he didn't like guests at meals, but he thought there wouldn't be enough duck. I told him it would do Wolfe good to go easy for a change, returned to the office, and found that Oster was back in the red leather chair, evidently on speaking terms, and Wolfe had a pen and pad of paper, taking notes. I interrupted to ask about drinks, got orders for a martini and a vodka on the rocks, and went to the kitchen to fill them.

Only two kinds of guests ever dine at that table: (a) men for whom Wolfe has personal feelings—there are eight altogether, and only two of them live in or near Near York—and (b) people who are involved in his current problem. With both kinds he makes a point of steering the table talk to subjects that he thinks the guests will be interested in; for him, as he once remarked, a guest is a jewel on the cushion of hospitality—a little fancy maybe, but a fine sentiment. As Fritz was serving the mussels I was wondering what it would be for those two. It was William Shakespeare. After the skimpy portions of mussels, in white wine with creamed butter and flour, had been commented on, Wolfe asked them if they had read the book by Rowse. They hadn't. But they were interested in Shakespeare? Oh, yes. Not many lawyers or professors would dare to say no. Of course they were familiar with *Othello*? They were. I cocked an eye at Wolfe. Surely it wasn't very tactful, with *those* dinner guests, to deliberately drag Othello in.

He swallowed his last bite of mussel. "There's an interesting point," he said. "A question. If the facts were established as they are presented in the play, could Iago, today in the State of New York, be legally charged with murder as an accessory, and be successfully prosecuted?"

I had to hand it to him. Unquestionably *Othello* concerned a subject in which they were interested, and putting the spot on Iago and a question of law made it discussable. They discussed it up one side and down the other. By the time the duck and trimmings had been disposed of, and Fritz had brought the fig soufflé, it looked to me as if Iago was on the ropes.

Fritz answers the doorbell during meals, so when it rang as I started on my soufflé I stayed put. It would be Cramer. Having read the report, he had come with questions, and they were welcome, because that was better than being invited to the DA's office. But it wasn't Cramer. The sound of voices came from the hall, Fritz's and another, and then another, not recognized. They stopped. There was no use trying to hear a door closing; not only does Fritz close doors quietly, but also Oster was talking. Fritz appeared, crossed the sill, and told Wolfe, "Two men and a woman, sir." Formerly he would have said two gentlemen and a lady, but Wolfe had stopped that. He went on, "Mr. and Mrs. Kenneth Brooke and Mr. Peter Vaughn. In the front room. I told them I thought you were engaged for the evening."

Wolfe looked at me. I nodded, "Her brother." He told Fritz he could bring the cheese and we would have coffee there instead of in the office, and forked a bite of soufflé. Oster asked, "Susan's brother?" and I said yes. He asked Wolfe, "You weren't expecting him?"

Wolfe swallowed the bite. "Not him specifically. I was rather expecting someone, this evening or tomorrow. The hook I baited." In the office he would have been smug, but not with guests, at the table. "I need another hour or so with you and Mr. Whipple, but it will have to wait. Perhaps Mr. Goodwin could call at your office in the morning?"

"I want to sit in on this. With these people."

"No, sir. We would probably start bickering in front of them I'll report it to you—at my discretion."

Fritz came with the cheese.

7

I stood in the alcove at the rear end of the hall, looking through the hole in the wall. On the alcove side it's just a hole, a rectangle with a sliding panel. On the office side it's covered by a picture of a waterfall which you can see through from the alcove. I was seeing through, for a preview of the two men and a woman whom Fritz had conducted to the office after Whipple and Oster had left. Wolfe, standing beside me, had already looked. Kenneth Brooke, in the red leather chair, had his head turned to face the other two, talking with them. He was chunky and solid, not slim like his sister. His wife, in the chair Paul Whipple had occupied before dinner, was a full-sized, positive blonde. I mean positive not as opposed to negative, but as opposed to vague. The other man, Peter Vaughn, of whom I had never heard, in a chair Fritz had moved up, was long and lanky, with a narrow bony face. Wolfe and I had been there, looking and listening, for six or seven minutes, but

the listening hadn't helped any. They were discussing a picture on the wall back of Wolfe's desk, not the waterfall. Vaughn
thought it was an unsigned Van Gogh, which it wasn't. It had
been painted by a man named McIntyre whom Wolfe had
once got out of a scrape.

Wolfe wiggled a finger, and I slid the noiseless panel shut.
He looked a question at me, had I ever seen any of them?
I shook my head, and he led the way to the office. Entering, he
detoured around Brooke to his desk, and I passed behind the
other two to mine. Before he sat he spoke. "I'm sorry you had
to wait. Usually I see callers only by appointment, but I make
exceptions. You are Susan Brooke's brother?"

Brooke nodded. "I am. My wife. Mr. Vaughn. Peter Vaughn.
We came—uh—on the spur of the moment. We appreciate—"

"That piece in the *Gazette*," Mrs. Brooke said. She talked
positive too. "We think you're right. We *know* you're right!"

"Indeed. That's gratifying." Wolfe moved a hand to indi-
cate me. "Mr. Goodwin, my confidential assistant. We are
both gratified. We thought you were probably going to say we
are wrong. How do you know we're right?"

They all spoke at once, or started to. Mrs. Brooke won. "*You*
tell *us*," she said, "how *you* know. Then we'll tell you." She
was making eyes at him. "They say ladies first, but we can
make exceptions too. This time gentlemen first."

Wolfe's lips were tight. I thought he was going to cut loose,
but he held it. He was almost polite. "But madam," he said,
"consider my position. I am engaged on behalf of a man who
may be put on trial for murder. He may be compelled to present his defense to a judge and jury. To disclose particulars
of that defense now to you, to anyone, would be to betray
him." He looked at the man beside her. "Who and what are

you, Mr. Vaughn? Are you on the staff of the district attorney?"

"No," Vaughn said, "nothing like that. I'm just a—a friend. I sell automobiles—Herons." He got a case from a pocket, extracted a card, and got up to hand it to Wolfe.

I gave myself a black mark. I had not only heard of him, I had seen him, casually. His father was Sam Vaughn, owner and operator of Heron Manhattan, Inc., which I visited at least once a year, to trade in Wolfe's sedan for a new one.

Wolfe's head turned. "And you, Mr. Brooke?"

"Does that matter? I'm Susan's brother. I'm an engineer by profession. Electronics. I assure you, we don't want you to betray anyone—quite the contrary."

"We want to know," his wife said, "if you know the truth, the truth about Susan."

Wolfe grunted. "So do I. I certainly don't know all of it. Perhaps you can help me. What fragment of the truth about her would you like me to know?"

"What she was like," Mrs. Brooke said.

"Her character, her personality," Brooke said.

"Her *quality*," Vaughn said. "She couldn't possibly have been . . . with a black man . . . that apartment. I was going to marry her."

"Indeed. She was engaged?"

"Well . . . it was understood. It had been for nearly two years. I was waiting until she had had enough of her—kink."

"Kink?"

"Well—caprice. Do-gooding."

"It wasn't just do-gooding," Mrs. Brooke declared. "I flatter myself that I do a little good myself sometimes. But Susan had to go all-out. Giving them money wasn't enough, and even working with them wasn't enough. She had to have that place right in the middle of the Harlem slums and even eat and sleep there sometimes."

Wolfe asked, "Were you ever there—that apartment?"

"Yes. I went with Mother Brooke—her mother. She insisted on seeing it. It was terrible—the neighborhood, the dirt and the smell, and the awful *people*. They don't want to be called niggers, but that's what they are. But the idea that Susan could be . . . with one of them . . . could have one of them with her in that apartment, that's absolutely absurd. She was a *lady*. She had a kink all right, but she was a lady. So you're perfectly right, that Dunbar Whipple didn't kill her. She was killed by some black hoodlum. Heaven knows there's enough of them."

Wolfe nodded. "Your logic seems sound. I understand the police have considered that possibility and reject it because valuables were there in plain sight, not taken, and Miss Brooke had not been sexually assaulted."

"That doesn't prove anything. Something scared him, some noise or something. Or he hadn't intended to kill her, and *that* scared him."

"Quite possible. As a conjecture, certainly admissible. But it will take more than a conjecture to clear Mr. Whipple; he was in the apartment; he had been there more than half an hour when the police arrived. The hoodlum theory is futile unless he is found and established. I'm not sure I understand your position. If, as you said, the idea that Miss Brooke 'could have one of them with her in that apartment' is absurd, how do you account for Mr. Whipple being there?"

"He went to ask her something or tell her something about her work. He lives only a few blocks away."

"But I understand that he went there frequently, that he has told the police that he and Miss Brooke were planning to be married."

"He's a liar," Vaughn said.

"That's absolutely absurd," Mrs. Brooke said.

"I don't understand *your* position," Brooke said. "According to the piece in the paper, you have good reason to believe that Dunbar Whipple is innocent, but you don't talk like it. You call the hoodlum theory futile. Will you tell us *why* you think he's innocent?"

"No, sir. Why do you? If you do."

"I'm not sure I do."

"Your wife said that you know I'm right."

"She should have said that we hope you're right." Brooke was forward in the chair, leaning forward. "When she showed me that piece in the paper, I said, 'Thank God.' My sister is dead, nothing can be done about that, but what's being printed and said about her—it's killing her mother. My mother. It's so ugly—that apartment and a Negro. If he didn't kill her and you can prove it, that will be different. Maybe he did go there just to talk about her work, and found her dead. That will be different. It might save my mother's life. I guess you know what I'm saying. I'm admitting that it's not impossible that my sister intended to marry a colored man—"

"*Kenneth!* Are you crazy?"

"I'm talking, Dolly." He stayed at Wolfe. "I wouldn't like it—who would?—but I admit it's possible. But they weren't married. Were they?"

"No."

"Then if he killed her it was—ugly. Sordid and ugly. But if you can prove he didn't kill her, that will be different. I'm repeating myself, but you know what I'm trying to say. It's the *murder* that counts. If someone else killed her, people will forget about Dunbar Whipple. Even my mother will forget about him—not really forget, I suppose, but it will be different.

So we want—I want to know why you say Whipple is innocent."

His wife had been trying to get a word in. She blurted it at him. "You're crazy, Kenneth! Susan would *not* have married a black man!"

"Oh, skip it, Dolly," he told her. "You know what you said just a month—"

"I was just talking!"

"Well, you said it." To Wolfe: "So I want to know. I not only want to know, I want to help. I know you get big fees, and I don't suppose Whipple or his father is very flush. If you'll tell me how it stands, I want to help."

"So do I," Vaughn said. "I don't think Susan— But that doesn't matter. My God, when I think . . ." He let it hang.

Wolfe shook his head. "Possibly you can help, but not with money. As for how it stands, it doesn't; it impends. I won't disclose the ground for my conclusion that Mr. Whipple is innocent, but it includes no inkling of the identity of the murderer. You might help with that; you were all close to her. If it was neither Mr. Whipple nor a hoodlum, who was it? Who is better off because she is dead? In mind or body or purse. That's always the question. Don't just shake your heads; consider it. Whose life is easier because hers is ended?"

"Nobody's," Brooke said.

"Pfui. Someone killed her, and someone who knew of that apartment. If you want to help me find him, search your memories. I have no memories; I start empty, and I'll start now. Mr. Brooke, where were you that evening between eight and nine o'clock?"

Brooke just stared at him.

"I'm quite serious," Wolfe said. "Sororicide is by no means unheard of. Where were you?"

"Good God," Brooke said, still staring.

"You're shocked. So would you be if you killed her. Where were you?"

"I was at my laboratory."

"From eight to nine?"

"From seven till nearly midnight. I was there when my wife phoned me about Susan."

"Were you alone?"

"No. Three others were there."

"Then the shock was bearable." Wolfe's head went right. "Mr. Vaughn?"

His bony jaw was set. "I resent this," he said.

"Of course you do. Anybody would. Where were you?"

"At my club. Harvard. Eating dinner and then watching a bridge game."

"From eight to nine?"

"Yes. And before and after."

"Then your resentment is also bearable. Mrs. Brooke?"

"I resent it too." Her face was showing color. "It's ridiculous."

"But not impertinent, if you want to help. Where were you?"

"I was at home. All evening."

"Alone?"

"No. My son was there."

"How old is your son?"

"Eight."

"Anyone else? A servant?"

"No. The maid was out." She moved abruptly and was on her feet. Her bag dropped to the floor, and Vaughn bent over to get it. "This is insulting," she said. "I'm surprised that you tolerate it, Kenneth. If he won't tell us anything, I'm sorry I suggested coming. Take me home." She moved.

Brooke's eyes went to Wolfe, to me, and to Vaughn. Apparently they were inviting a suggestion but got none. His wife had stepped to the door. Rising, he told Wolfe, "I'm in the phone book, both my laboratory and my home. When I said I want to help I meant it. Come on, Peter."

Vaughn thought he was going to say something but vetoed it, and because of his hesitation I reached the hall ahead of them. Mrs. Brooke was at the rack, getting her coat, and I went and offered a hand. She ignored it, gave me a withering look, stood until the men approached, and said, "Hold my coat, Kenneth." I opened the door wide, quick, to let the cold air hit her before she got it on. As they went out and I shut the door I decided to see the eight-year-old son in the near future and ask him what time he had gone to bed on Monday, March 2. No woman can throw a pie at me and keep my good will.

I went to the office and told Wolfe, "Okay, Dolly Brooke killed her because she was going to marry a quote nigger unquote, and how do we prove it?"

He frowned. "I have told you not to use that word in my hearing."

"I was merely quoting. It isn't—"

"Shut up. I mean the word 'unquote' and you know it."

I took a good stretch and an unpatted yawn. "Too much sitting and no walk. Six hours at the typewriter. Mrs. Brooke deliberately insulted me on the way out. It was at her suggestion that they came. She wanted to find out how much you knew. A month ago she told her husband that she knew or suspected that Susan was going to marry a quote nigger end of quotation. She knew where the apartment was; she had been there. She had to kill Susan; it wouldn't have solved the problem to kill Dunbar because Susan would merely have

picked another one—the way she saw it. The alibi is piddling.
For something as important as a murder you couldn't be
blamed for leaving a boy in bed asleep, or even for putting
just a touch of pentobarbital sodium in his milk. Or Mother
Brooke came and baby-sat, knowing or unknowing. Filicide
is no more unheard of than sororicide. What have I left out?"

"Three little points. She said Susan Brooke was a lady. She
didn't consider her one, and doesn't. She knew that Mr. Whipple lives not far from that apartment. She dropped her bag
when she stood up. Where does she live?"

I went to my desk, got the Manhattan book, and found the
page. "Park Avenue in the Sixties. Sixty-seventh or -eighth."

"How would she have gone?"

"Probably a taxi. Possibly her own car if she has one."

"Get Saul. Has she a car, and if so, did she use it that evening. Your notebook."

I objected. Saul Panzer's rate was ten dollars an hour, plus
expenses, and this was on the house. I asked politely, "Am I
crippled?"

"You have another errand—Mr. Oster and Mr. Whipple. Your
notebook. For tomorrow's paper, one will do, the *Gazette*. Single column, say two inches. Headed 'A cabdriver,' fourteen-
point, boldface. Following, eleven-point standard: 'took an
attractive well-dressed woman, comma, around thirty, comma,
from the Sixties to One Hundred and Twenty-eighth Street
early in the evening of Monday, comma, March second. It will
be to his advantage to communicate with me.' Below, my name
and address and telephone number. To run three days, tomorrow, Monday, and Tuesday. Any comment?"

"One. *East* Sixties."

"Insert it."

"She may spot it. Does that matter?"

"No. If she's open to menace, the more she's stirred the better. Your notebook. Questions for Mr. Oster and Mr. Whipple. We don't want an army here. Only those who—"

"I'll get the ad in first." I got the phone and dialed.

8

It was a lousy weekend. Nothing went right. Nothing went exactly wrong either, but you can say that if you just go to bed and don't get up.

My Saturday morning date with Oster and Whipple was canceled because Oster was called to Washington for a parley at the Department of Justice. He might be back Sunday night. Saul Panzer is the best free-lance operative who ever stopped a closing door with his foot, but even Saul was stymied when he learned that the man who had been on duty that Monday evening at the garage where the Kenneth Brookes kept their two Herons was off somewhere for the weekend, nobody knew where. At four o'clock Saturday afternoon I was invited to the DA's office to discuss some selected items in the report I had delivered to Cramer, and was kept so long by an assistant district attorney named Mandel, who would enjoy looking at me through bars with him on the outside, that I was two hours late for a dancing date with friends at the Flamingo. Lon Cohen phoned once Saturday and twice Sunday. Some brainy journalist, maybe Lon himself, having seen the ad, had recalled the fact that Susan Brooke's married brother lived in the East Sixties, and of course 128th Street was obvious, and Lon wanted to know what gave. I stalled him off Saturday, but he called twice Sunday to ask if the hackie had shown. He hadn't. Not a peep.

A lousy weekend.

I finally got to Oster early Monday afternoon, at the office of the ROCC, a whole floor of a building on 39th Street near Lexington Avenue. It wasn't lavish, but neither was it seedy. I was a little surprised to see that the switchboard girl, who doubled in reception, was my color, even a little lighter—a middle-aged female, hair showing some gray, with a chin and a half and a long thin nose, which didn't fit. I learned later that of the total office staff of thirty-four, five were white, and of the five whites, four were volunteers, what Dolly Brooke would call do-gooders.

Oster's room was small, one window, but after a few words he took me down the hall to the corner room of the executive director, Thomas Henchy, and it was quite a chamber, with a few dozen photographs on the walls where the cabinets and shelves left room. I had seen Henchy on television a couple of times, and so have you probably—broad shoulders, cheeks a little pudgy but not flabby, short neck. Color, strong coffee with one teaspoon of cream. He got up to shake hands, and I took a little care with the grip. Men with short necks are apt to be knuckle-crushers.

When I left, more than an hour later, the program for the evening was set, with no hard feelings. I had explained that when Wolfe had said "the entire staff" he hadn't meant it literally. He wanted to see only those who, because of their contacts or relations with Susan or Dunbar, or both, might possibly be able to supply useful information; and the selection would be up to them, Oster and Henchy, in discussion with me. That was satisfactory, and we proceeded to discuss. I had a list in my pocket when I left, and when I got back to the office I typed it for Wolfe:

THOMAS HENCHY, around 50, executive director. He was courteous but not cordial. He knows it's doing ROCC a lot of harm and he hates it. Possibly thinks Whipple killed her.

HAROLD R. OSTER, Counsel. He had evidently told Henchy that a conference at our office was his idea, and I didn't spoil it.

ADAM EWING, around 40, colored, in charge of public relations, worked closely with Whipple. I met him. Smart and very earnest. Thinks he knows everything, and possibly does. Chips on both shoulders. Light caramel.

CASS FAISON, 45, colored, in charge of fund-raising. Susan Brooke worked under him. I met him. They don't come any blacker. Turns his grin on and off. I wouldn't be surprised if he liked Susan and doesn't like Dunbar. No innuendo intended.

MISS RAE KALLMAN, about Susan's age, white. She helped Susan arrange meetings and parties. Susan recruited her and paid her personally, but she is staying on for a while. Didn't meet her. I got the impression that she didn't approve of Susan's cottoning to Dunbar. I didn't go into points like that since I wasn't supposed to, but I got the impression.

MISS BETH TIGER, colored, 21, stenographer. Only Henchy has a secretary, they're shorthanded, but she took all of Dunbar's dictation. Another impression, from a comment by Henchy: she would have been willing to take more than dictation from Dunbar. Didn't meet her.

Miss Maud Jordan, white, 50 or more, switchboard and receptionist. She is included chiefly because she took the phone call from Susan that afternoon and put the message on Dunbar's desk that Susan couldn't get to the apartment until nine o'clock. She's a volunteer, hipped on civil rights, another dogooder, evidently with a private pile since she takes no pay and Henchy mentioned that she gave $500 to the fund for Medgar Evers's children. I saw her entering and leaving. An old maid, spinster to you, who had to be hipped on something and happened to stumble on civil rights or maybe wrongs. My impression, based on my infallible understanding of women under 90.

All of them knew about the apartment. Henchy, Ewing, Faison, and Kallman knew where it was. Oster says he didn't. Jordan knew the phone number. Tiger, I don't know.

When Wolfe came down from the plant rooms at six o'clock he picked it up, read it twice, scowled at it for two minutes, put it in a drawer, and picked up his current book. Not Rowse on Shakespeare; *The Minister and the Choir Singer*, by a lawyer named Kunstler. I had read it and recommended it. At dinner we discussed it and agreed that the New York Police Department and district attorney's office had never made such an awful mess of a case and never would.

The evening didn't start off any too well. When four or more are coming for an after-dinner session I equip a portable bar in the kitchen and wheel it into the office, and it was there, by the bookshelves to the left of the safe, when the first one arrived; but twenty minutes later, when they had all come and been seated, and Wolfe entered, I had made no sales. That was remarkable. Out of eight people, at nine o'clock in the evening, you would expect at least two or three to be thirsty enough or bushed enough to want a drink, but they all said no. It couldn't have been because of my manners, offering to serve people of an inferior race. First, two of them were white, and second, when I consider myself superior to anyone, as I frequently do, I need a better reason than his skin.

The seating was segregated, not by color but by sex. Wolfe had told me to put Whipple, the client, in the red leather chair, and since he had arrived before Oster there had been no clash. In the front row of yellow chairs Oster was at the far end from me, then Henchy, Ewing, public relations, and Faison, fund-raising. In the back row were Rae Kallman, Maud Jordan, and Beth Tiger. It was my first sight of the Misses Kallman and Tiger. Kallman, who had more lipstick than necessary on her full lips, would probably be plump in a few years, but now she was just nice and curvy. Tiger was one of those specimens who cannot be properly introduced by details. I'll mention that her skin was about the color of an old solid-gold bowl Wolfe has in his room which he won't allow Fritz to clean, that if she had been Cleopatra instead of what's-her-name I wouldn't have missed that movie, and that I had a problem with my eyes all evening, since with a group there I am supposed to watch expressions and movements. It was especially difficult because Miss Tiger, nearest me in the back row, was at an angle to my right. My mistake.

It was ten past nine when I buzzed the kitchen on the house phone to tell Wolfe they were all there, and in a minute he entered, circled around Whipple to his desk, and stood while I pronounced names. To each one he nodded, his usual eighth-of-an-inch nod, then turned to me and demanded, "The refreshments, Archie?"

"Offered," I said, "and declined."

"Indeed. Beer for me, please." As I rose he turned to the client. "Mr. Whipple, that evening at Upshur Pavilion you took ginger ale."

Whipple's eyes widened. "You remember *that*?"

"Certainly. But the other day you had a martini. Will it be ginger ale now? I'm having beer and invite you to join me— to your taste."

"All right, I will. Scotch and soda."

"Mr. Henchy?"

The executive director objected. "It takes time."

"Come, sir, is time really so precious? Mine isn't. If yours is, all the more tempting to steal a little."

Henchy's eyes smiled, but he wouldn't let his mouth chip in. "It's a point," he conceded. "Bourbon on the rocks."

With the boss sold, the others came along. Rae Kallman offered to help, and that reduced the loss of time. The only holdout was Maud Jordan, and when the others had been served she made it unanimous by asking for a glass of water. I took gin and tonic because Miss Tiger did. I believe in fellowship.

Wolfe put his glass down, half empty, and sent his eyes left, then right. "I suppose all of you know that I am proceeding on the premise that Dunbar Whipple was not implicated in the murder of Susan Brooke. That needs no discussion unless one or more of you challenge it. Do you?"

Some shook their heads and some said no.

"Let's make it clear. Will all of you who agree with me on that point please raise your hands?"

As Miss Tiger raised hers, her head turned right. Checking. Two of them, Cass Faison and Rae Kallman, were a little slow. Henchy moved only his forearm, to a forty-five degree angle. "But we're not the jury and you're not the judge," Adam Ewing said.

"The intention, Mr. Ewing, is that it shall never get to a judge and jury." Wolfe's eyes went left and right. "Of course all of you have been questioned separately by the police, except Mr. Oster. For our joint purpose, to clear Mr. Whipple, this joint discussion was preferable, but to avoid confusion let's start with each of you singly. But attend, please; if any of you hear a statement made by another that you challenge or question, say so at once. Intervene. Don't let it pass. Is that understood?"

No one said it wasn't.

"Very well. Mr. Goodwin reports that all of you knew of that apartment, and I am assuming that all of you knew where it was, again excepting Mr. Oster. Any comment?"

"I did." Beth Tiger.

"I didn't." Maud Jordan. "I knew the phone number, I knew it was in Harlem, but I didn't know the address."

"Nevertheless, I am assuming that you did. You, Miss Jordan, knowing the phone number, could easily have learned the address. Actually, Mr. Oster, I am not excepting even you. However unlikely it may be that one of you went there and killed Susan Brooke, it is by no means unthinkable. The possibility is in my mind, naturally, but at the back. The police have questioned you regarding your whereabouts that evening, but I won't. If later something points to one of you, we'll see. An alibi is rarely unimpeachable. What I—"

"Just a minute," Henchy cut in. "When you asked if we agreed that Whipple didn't kill her I put my hand up. If you ask if we think no one in this room killed her, I'll put it up again." He jerked forward and hit his knee with a fist. "If you want to clear Whipple, all right, I hope you do, but you're not going to do it by putting it on one of us!"

"I'm not going to 'put it on' anybody, Mr. Henchy. I'm going to find the man who 'put it on' himself a week ago." Wolfe looked at the clock. "Almost precisely a week ago. I'll begin with you, Miss Jordan."

"Me?" Her mouth stayed open.

"Yes. A vital point is the telephone call by Miss Brooke and the message Mr. Whipple found on his desk shortly before six o'clock. Did you put the message on his desk?"

"Yes. I have told the police all about it."

"Certainly. You received the call by Miss Brooke?"

"Yes. At the switchboard."

"What time did the call come?"

"At a quarter past five. I put it on the slip, five-fifteen."

"What did she say?"

"She wanted to speak to Mr. Whipple, and I said he was in a conference, and she told me to tell him that she couldn't get there until nine o'clock or a little later."

"Can you give me her exact words?"

She frowned, making her long thin nose look longer. "I have tried to. To the police. When I said, 'Rights of Citizens Committee,' she said, 'This is Susan, Maud. Please give me Mr. Whipple.' I said, 'He's in conference in Mr. Henchy's room, the people from Philadelphia and Chicago,' and she said, 'Then will you tell him I won't be able to get there until nine or a little later?' I said, 'I leave at five-thirty. Will it be all right if I leave a message on his desk?' and she said, 'Yes, of course.' She hung up."

Wolfe glanced at me, saw that I was getting it in the notebook, and returned to her. "On the next point it's regrettable that you have already been questioned by the police, but it can't be helped. Probably it is now fixed in your mind, but I must ask anyway. How sure are you that it was Miss Brooke speaking?"

She nodded. "It was her. They wanted to know if I would swear to it on the witness stand, and I told them I couldn't swear it was her because I didn't *see* her, but if it was someone

imitating her voice I would have to hear her do it again before
I would believe it."

"Her using your first name was customary?"

"Yes."

"At the time, as she spoke, you noticed no oddity whatever?"

"No. Of course not."

"You say 'of course,' Miss Jordan, because your mind is now
fixed. You have committed yourself. That's a pity, since I have
no ground at present for a demur." Wolfe looked right and left.
"This is patently crucial. If only I had spoken with Miss Jordan
before she committed herself to the police. If I assume that
Mr. Whipple is innocent, as I do, I must also assume that Miss
Brooke did not make that telephone call. Either that or—"

"No," Oster said, "not necessarily. She might have made it
and got there earlier than she expected to. The question is, did
she get there before Whipple, and how long before, and on that
there is evidence. She was in that neighborhood, at a package
store and a delicatessen, before eight o'clock. So she was there
before Whipple came, probably about an hour, and that's the
point."

Wolfe was shaking his head. "That is *not* the point. Take the
murderer. Since he was not Dunbar Whipple, call him X. He
knew about the apartment and that Miss Brooke would be
there early in the evening, so in all likelihood he knew that
Mr. Whipple would be there too. Would he have entered—
presumably admitted by Miss Brooke—and clubbed her to
death if Whipple might come at any moment? I don't believe it.
He was done for if Whipple arrived, not only while he was in
the apartment, but while he was descending two flights of
stairs and leaving the building. I reject it. I think X knew that
telephone call had been made and that Whipple would not
come until later. Either he knew that Miss Brooke had made

the call, or he had himself made it, imitating Miss Brooke's voice—in which case it is she, not he—or he had a confederate who made the call. So, Miss Jordan, we need you for another point. Who besides you knew of that call?"

"Nobody." The crease in her chin and a half was deeper because her jaw was set. "I told you, I took it at the switchboard."

"Did you mention it to anyone?"

"No."

"It came at five-fifteen. Did you write the message on the slip immediately?"

"Yes. I would be leaving in a few minutes."

"When did you take the message to Mr. Whipple's room?"

"When I left. Just before I left."

"Could anyone have seen it there at the switchboard, on your desk or table?"

"No. There was nobody there until just before I left, and then I had it in my hand."

"Was anyone in Mr. Whipple's room when you went there with it?"

"No."

"You put it on his desk in plain sight?"

"Of course. So he would see it. Under a paperweight."

Wolfe's eyes went to the executive director. "Mr. Henchy. Dunbar Whipple told me that the conference ended a little after six o'clock. Is that correct?"

Henchy nodded. "Five or ten minutes after six."

"Was anyone here present, besides you, at the conference?"

"Yes. Mr. Ewing, Mr. Faison, and Mr. Oster."

"Did any of you four leave the room after half past five, before the conference ended?"

Adam Ewing exploded. "This is poppycock! *You* grilling *us!*"

Wolfe regarded him. "I believe, sir, you are in charge of what is called 'public relations' for your organization. Surely it is in its interest, if Dunbar Whipple is innocent, to have the murderer exposed and dealt with as soon as possible. You don't want it to be someone now in this room, and neither do I. I have contributed to the Rights of Citizens Committee—how much, Archie?"

"Fifty dollars a year for the past seven years." I slanted a glance at Miss Tiger to see if she was impressed. Apparently not.

"But that telephone call is a vital point, and if Miss Brooke made it I must know who might have learned about it. Mr. Oster, I told you that if you wished to object to anything I say, you have a tongue. Do you object to this?"

"No," the lawyer said. "I think it's immaterial, but this isn't a courtroom."

"It *may* be immaterial. Shall I repeat the question, Mr. Henchy?"

"No. I'll answer for myself. I was in the room continuously until the conference ended."

"I wasn't," Cass Faison said. I had him in profile, and the light glancing off his black cheek gave it a high gloss. "I had an appointment and left about a quarter to six."

"Did you enter Mr. Whipple's room?"

"No. I want to say, I doubt if Dunbar Whipple killed her, not with a club like that, but if he did I hope he gets the chair. Whoever killed Susan Brooke, whether he's here in this room or not, I hope he gets it."

"So do I," Ewing snapped. "We all do." He aimed his sharp brown eyes at Wolfe. "If Oster doesn't object, I don't. I was out of the room for a few minutes, to go to the men's room, and it may have been after five-thirty. I don't know. I didn't enter

Whipple's room, and I knew nothing about the phone call or message."

"Then I need not grill you. Mr. Oster, if you don't object, you were at the conference?"

"Yes. Like Mr. Henchy, continuously. I learned about the phone call from Miss Jordan the next morning."

"Miss Kallman. Did you enter Mr. Whipple's room during the specified period?"

"I wasn't there." She put her glass down on the stand between her chair and Maud Jordan's. "I wasn't at the office much. I was usually out most of the day. I was that day." All past tense, though Henchy had told me she was staying on. Probably immaterial.

"Were you with Miss Brooke that afternoon?"

"No. I was in Brooklyn, seeing some people. She had a five-o'clock meeting with some students at NYU."

"When did you last see her?"

"That morning at the office. We often met there, especially Mondays, to plan for the day. But I think I should tell you—" She stopped.

"Yes?"

"I told the police. I often phoned her in the evening, if there was anything to report or ask about. That morning she told me she would be at the Wadsworth number that evening, and about half past eight, a little after half past, I dialed that number, but there was no answer."

"The number of the apartment on One Hundred and Twenty-eighth Street?"

"Yes."

Wolfe grunted. "The police probably assume she hadn't arrived. I assume she was dead. Then you didn't know of her call to the office at five-fifteen?"

"No."

"You, Miss Tiger?"

Now it was in order to look at her straight, and that was a relief. I had never seen a package, anywhere, more glomable. With my eyes, which are good, free to stick, I decided that her long lashes were home-grown. She told Wolfe, in a tight low-pitched voice, "I saw the message. There on his desk. When I took some letters for him to sign."

Wolfe's eyes, on her, were precisely the same as when they were on Maud Jordan. Yet he's a man. "Indeed," he said. "Then you might as well tell me where you spent the next three hours."

She didn't object. "I was there until half past six, with the letters he had signed. Then I ate something in a restaurant. Then I went home and studied."

"Studied?"

"Economics. I'm going to be an economist. Do you know where I live?"

"No. Where?"

"In that same building on One Hundred and Twenty-eighth Street. I have a room on the fourth floor. When Susan Brooke wanted to find an apartment in Harlem she asked me if I knew of any, and that one on the third floor happened to be vacant. If I had known . . ."

"Yes?"

"Nothing."

"You were in your room alone that evening?"

"Yes. From eight o'clock on. For a while the police thought I killed her. I didn't. I never left the room, even after the police came. They wanted to take me somewhere to be questioned, but I refused to go unless they arrested me, and they didn't. I know the rights of a citizen. I went to the district attorney's office the next day. I want to ask you something. I have asked Mr. Oster but I'm not sure he's right, and I want to ask you. If a person says she committed a murder she can't be convicted just because she says she did it. There has to be some evidence. Is that true?"

"Yes."

"Then I'll be a witness and say I killed her. Mr. Oster says I would be cross-examined and discredited, but I don't believe it. I can answer any question they ask me. Then he wouldn't be convicted, and I couldn't be. Isn't that true?"

Wolfe's lips were tight. He took a deep breath. Henchy and Oster both said something, but he ignored them. He took another breath. "You deserve a frank answer, madam. You are either a female daredevil or a jenny. If you killed her you would be risking disaster; if you didn't kill her, you would be inviting derision. If you killed her, I advise you to say nothing to anyone, particularly me; if you didn't, help me find the man who did. Or woman."

"I didn't kill her."

"Then don't be a lackwit. Is that apartment on the third floor directly below your room?"

"No, it's in the rear. I'm at the front."

"Did you hear any unusual sounds that evening between eight and nine o'clock?"

"No. The first unusual sounds were after the police came."

"I presume Mr. Whipple knew that you lived there, on the floor above. He told me that he stayed in the apartment until the police arrived—more than half an hour after he discovered the body. It might be thought that at that crisis the impulse to confer with an associate, a friend, so near at hand, would be irresistible. But he didn't?"

"No, he didn't. I'm glad he didn't."

"Why glad?"

"Because I know—I think I would have gone down and put my fingerprints on the club."

"Pfui. You think he would have let you?"

"He wouldn't have known. He would have stayed in my room."

"Then I'm as glad as you are that he didn't go to you. This job is knotty enough without that. Archie, the glasses are empty."

As I went to the bar for a bottle of beer and took it to him, a couple of them made remarks that can be skipped, and Miss Kallman got up to help. They all took refills except Miss Tiger. Her glass was still two-thirds full, with the ice gone, but she didn't even want more ice. By the time the others had been served, Henchy had downed most of his refill, and I put the bourbon bottle on the stand between him and Oster, and he emptied his glass, picked up the bottle, and poured. It was twelve-year-old Big Sandy, which is worth stealing a little time for. As for me, I went to the kitchen and got a glass of milk. I would like to be loyal to Miss Tiger and say that what she didn't want I didn't want, but the truth is that ever since the time I missed an important point because I had had four martinis to be sociable I have limited myself to one dose when I'm working. When I returned to the office with the milk, Oster was speaking:

". . . so I didn't object, but it was immaterial. What does it matter who knew of the phone call or the message? Say I saw the message on Whipple's desk. I would know that he probably wouldn't be at the apartment until nine o'clock, but I would also know that Susan wouldn't either. Therefore I wouldn't go there at eight o'clock, to see her or kill her before Whipple came. Therefore it's immaterial."

Wolfe nodded and put his glass down. "Obviously, if it were that simple, but it isn't. The telling point is that if you saw the message you knew it was fairly certain that Whipple wouldn't arrive until around nine o'clock. During the two hours between six and eight you might have learned—no matter how, there are various possibilities—that Miss Brooke had changed her plans and would get there earlier. You might even have met her, by design or accident, and gone to the apartment with her on some pretext."

"Possible." Oster pursed his lips, considering it, then jerked his chin up, and I thought he had decided to take charge. But he only said, "Are you going to ignore the fact that someone besides Miss Tiger knew about the message?"

"No. I was keeping that for later, but if you want it now . . ." Wolfe's eyes went right. "He means you, of course, Miss Jordan. You left the office at five-thirty. How did you spend the next three hours?"

There was a flash in her eyes that I didn't know she had. "I didn't spend it *killing* anybody," she snapped.

"Good. Nor, I hope, at any other mischief. You must have told the police; why not tell me? Miss Tiger did."

"Oh, I'll tell you. What I told them. I stopped at three places on the way home to buy some things—a book, and stockings, and cream and bread and pickles—and went home and cooked my supper, and ate it, and read the book until I went to bed."

"What book?"

"*The Group.* By Mary McCarthy."

Wolfe made a face. He had read two chapters and ditched it. "Where do you live?"

"I have a little apartment on Forty-seventh Street near Lexington Avenue. I'm alone in the world."

"At least you're aware of it. Many people aren't. Now,

madam, a point we haven't dealt with yet. What is your feeling about a Negro marrying a white woman?"

The flash again. "That's none of your business."

"My personal business, no. But it's of urgent concern to me as the man hired by Mr. Whipple to find out who killed Susan Brooke. If you have a reason to refuse to answer, I—"

"I have no *reason*. It's impertinent, that's all. Everyone at the ROCC knows how I feel about it, and other people too. Anyone has a right to marry anyone. It's a *right*. Marrying the woman of your choice or the man of your choice is a God-given right."

"Then you didn't resent the relationship between Mr. Whipple and Miss Brooke?"

"It was none of my business. Except I thought if she married him all her money would be devoted to the cause, and that would be wonderful."

"We all thought that," Cass Faison said. "Or nearly all."

"Not me," Adam Ewing said. "I'm the exception. From the public-relations viewpoint, I thought it would be unwise. I *knew* it would be. I can say here exactly how I feel, I've said it to bigger crowds than this, and some of them mixed. Sex and money are at the bottom of all the opposition to civil rights, just as they're at the bottom of everything else. Black and white marrying is like a red rag to a bull." He gestured. "But I wouldn't kill a woman to stop it. I'm not a killer. Let the opposition do the killing."

"I'm an exception too," Beth Tiger said. "I didn't think it would be wonderful."

"You agree with Mr. Ewing?"

"That's not it. I just say I didn't think it would be wonderful. That's all I'm going to say."

"Miss Kallman?"

Rae Kallman shook her head but didn't open her mouth. "Does that mean you disapproved?"

"No. It means I said to Susan what I had to say. She was the only one I had any right to say it to, and she's dead. The police couldn't drag it out of me, and neither can you."

"Then I won't try. Mr. Henchy?"

He cleared his throat. If I had been with him on the bourbon, I would have had to clear mine twice. "On the whole, I approved. Marriage is a very personal matter, but insofar as the interests of the organization were concerned I was in agreement with Mr. Faison. I thought the advantages would outweigh the disadvantages. In my position I must be realistic. Miss Brooke was a very wealthy woman." He reached for his glass.

"And you, Mr. Oster?"

The lawyer cocked his head. "You know, Wolfe, I'm sitting here taking it in. I'm giving you all the rope you want. But asking *me* how I feel about a Negro marrying a white woman —how remote can you get? I'll send you a copy of a magazine with an article I wrote four years ago. Every civilized strain of mankind on earth is the result of interbreeding. Evidently nature approves of it, so I do. I'm not going to indict nature."

"You had no special feeling about this particular instance?"

"Certainly not."

Wolfe poured beer, emptying the bottle. He put it down and looked left and right. "I admit," he said, "that much of what has been said has probably been a waste of time. I hope it has, for in spite of Miss Jordan's conviction I will not discard the guess that the telephone call was not made by Miss Brooke. I like it; its attractions are many and manifest." His eyes settled on my assistant bartender. "Miss Kallman, you said that

Miss Brooke had a five-o'clock meeting that day. Do you know where it was to be held?"

"It was at NYU, but I don't know which building or room."

"Can you find out?"

"Yes, easily."

"And the names of some of the people who were there?"

"I can tell you one name now. Bill Magnus. William Magnus. I have his address and phone number at the office. He could give you other names. I saw him last week. Many people have wanted to see me, since Susan—"

"The meeting took place and Miss Brooke was there?"

"Yes."

"Can Mr. Goodwin call you in the morning and get Mr. Magnus's address?"

"I had better call him. I'm never sure just when I'll be there."

"Will you do so?"

"Yes, of course."

"I've talked with Magnus," Oster said. "So have the police, naturally. You won't get anything conclusive, one way or the other."

Wolfe was swallowing beer. It was turning into a big beer night, three bottles instead of the usual one or two. He put the glass down and licked his lips. "There's always a chance of a hint, and Mr. Goodwin is good at hints. I can't say about you, but the police were surely satisfied to have it that Miss Brooke made that call, and I am not. If there's any—"

The phone rang, and I turned and got it. "Nero Wolfe's resi—"

"Saul, Archie. I've got a slice of maybe bacon."

"We could use some. We have company. Hold it."

"Sure."

I pressed a button, rose, detoured around the chairs, passing only eight inches from Miss Tiger's shoulder, went to the kitchen, and got at the phone on my breakfast table.

"Goodwin speaking."

"You sound more like Lieutenant Rowcliff."

"I do not. I don't stutter. Well?"

"It cost twenty bucks. Some garage attendants have delusions of grandeur. The Brookes have two cars, Herons, a sedan and a station wagon. Mr. Brooke uses the wagon every day, Monday to Friday; he drives to his laboratory in Brooklyn. He returned it to the garage that Monday evening, March second, around midnight. Mrs. Brooke came and got the sedan that evening between seven and eight. His guess is about a quarter to eight. She brought it back about an hour later, maybe an hour and a half."

"Saul, I love you, except at the poker table. Will he tell her?"

"No. He would deny he told me. I had to swear he wouldn't be quoted. I merely wanted the information, you know?"

"Yeah. How much chance is there that he made it up to give you your money's worth?"

"Now listen. Wouldn't I have said so?"

"I withdraw it. Of course you have the color and license number. How was she dressed?"

"He didn't notice."

With Saul you don't ask silly questions, such as was she alone going and coming. "All right," I said, "she may not be a murderer, but she's a damn liar. He's finishing up a three-bottle session with an integrated audience. One of them is a brown girl, golden brown, whom you'd better never meet if you don't want to be glued. I don't want to be rude, but I have to get back in there. Where are you?"

"A booth. Sixty-fourth and Lexington."

"Where will you be?"

"Home in bed. It's nearly midnight."

"If we don't ring you tonight we will in the morning. Stand by, huh?"

He said he would. I cradled the phone and sat a minute looking at it. It was the kind of thing Wolfe hates and I'm not too fond of myself. Trying to find someone or ones who had seen that car in Harlem that evening, granting it had been there, was a job for an army. Facing her with it as a known fact without naming the source would be a waste of breath. I got up, said a word aloud that needn't be in the record, went to the hall, and found that the party was over. Two of them were on their way to the front, and the others were filing out of the office, all but Paul Whipple, who was having a word with Wolfe at his desk.

I went to help with coats and hats, and deliberately selected Maud Jordan's, letting one of the others serve Miss Tiger. I didn't want to give her the impression that I was at her beck, let alone her call. Then Paul Whipple came, and I had his ready for him. He was the last one out.

When I went to the office Wolfe had his reading light on and had opened *The Minister and the Choir Singer*. That was as it should be; he would stay to keep me company while I took things out and straightened up. To go up to bed, leaving the mess to me, would sort of imply that I was merely a menial, so he stayed to collaborate. As I entered he looked a question.

I nodded. "Saul. Mrs. Brooke forgets things. Monday evening, March second, around a quarter to eight, she got her car from the garage and brought it back an hour or more later. Saul shelled out twenty dollars to the garage attendant and promised not to reveal the source. No one with her."

He growled. "Confound her."

"Yes, sir. I told Saul we'd ring him tonight or in the morning. Any instructions?"

"It's past bedtime. Ask Saul to come at eleven. If Miss Kallman hasn't called by ten o'clock you should call her."

"Right. Do you want to see Magnus?"

"No. You will."

Meaning he only did the tricky ones. He raised his book, and I started collecting glasses. Miss Tiger's was still two-thirds full. Wasting good gin, Follansbee's.

9

A problem like Dolly Brooke's lie is plain ornery. Even if we could get the garage man to play along and he said it to her face, a big if, she could say that he was mistaken, it had been another evening, or that she had gone on a personal errand which she preferred to keep to herself; and if she had actually driven to 128th Street and killed Susan Brooke it wouldn't help any to let her know we had caught her in a lie just to show her how smart we were. You might like to know how Nero Wolfe would handle such a problem, but I can't tell you in this particular case because he didn't handle it at all. Luck did. The luck rang the doorbell of the old brownstone at five minutes to ten Tuesday morning.

But first William Magnus. Rae Kallman phoned while I was at my breakfast table in the kitchen, on my fourth homemade Creole pork sausage and my third Creole fritter. She had discovered that she had Magnus's phone number in a notebook at home, and she had called him early, to get him before he left. By now he had gone for a day at school. He would have no free time until four-thirty, and we could expect him a little before five. As I resumed with the sausage and fritters I considered the fact that Miss Kallman was cooperating beyond the call of duty; she had promised only to supply his address and phone number. Sometimes—not often, but it does happen—such a little detail has a point. Had she wanted to brief him, and if so, why? A corner of my mind was still considering it in the office as I opened the morning mail.

When luck rang the doorbell at 9:55 I didn't know it was luck, even after I went to the hall and saw him on the stoop. Peter Vaughn was merely the long and lanky specimen who was still trying to hang onto the notion that he had been going to marry Susan Brooke after she got rid of her kink. As a candidate for the tag, at least 100 to 1. But when I opened the door and saw him closer, it was obvious that something really sharp was biting him. His bony face looked even narrower, and he had to unclamp his jaw to speak, to say that he knew Wolfe wasn't available at that hour, but he would rather see me anyway. That was grease, or it wasn't. I took him to the office and moved a chair up to face mine. He sat, clamped his jaw again, and rubbed his eyes, which were red and puffy, first with his fingertips and then with the heels of his palms.

"I haven't slept for four nights," he said.

I nodded. "You look it." Four nights had passed since he had been there with his future in-laws. If I had been Wolfe I would have asked if he had eaten. Being me, I asked, "How about a drink? Or coffee?"

"No, thanks." He tried to eye me, but it was mostly blinks. "I know a couple of men who know about you, and it's because of what they said that I would rather see you than Wolfe. They said you're tough but straight, and you're more human than Wolfe."

"At least I try."

He didn't hear it. He was in the kind of condition when you're so concentrated on what you want to say that nothing anyone else says can get in.

"I'm in one hell of a squeeze," he said. "I'm stuck. First I ought to tell you, I don't owe Kenneth and Dolly Brooke anything. They don't owe me anything, either. I met them through Susan, about three years ago. I only knew them, I only kept knowing them and seeing them, on account of her. So I don't feel— Wait a minute. I didn't say this is confidential. It is."

I shook my head. "Not if it connects up with murder. I mustn't make liars of the men who told you I'm straight. Put it this way: nothing you tell me will be disclosed unless it has to be in order to nail a murderer. Everything else is, and will stay, confidential. Is that plain?"

"Yes." A muscle at the side of his neck was twitching. "I suppose . . . All right. I admit I'm thinking of *me*. I lied to the police."

"If I had a dime for every lie I've told them I'd be on my yacht in the Caribbean. What is it you don't feel?"

"What?"

"You said, 'I don't feel,' and stopped."

"I don't— Oh. Yes. I don't feel that there's any question of *loyalty*. I don't owe them any loyalty. I said I'm thinking of me, and I am, but the trouble is I have a conscience. That's an old-fashioned word, and I'm not religious, but I don't know what else to call it. That's why I haven't been able to sleep. What I can't stand— You remember, when we were here Friday evening, we tried to get Wolfe to tell us why he thinks that man is innocent, and he wouldn't. I want you to tell me why. Confidentially. Just for me."

It was beginning to sound promising. What was eating him might be something we could use, and the odds had at least doubled that he wasn't it. I made an effort. "If it would get you some sleep," I said, "I wish I could tell you. But if I did, people would no longer call me straight. Dunbar Whipple is Nero Wolfe's client, and I work for Nero Wolfe. But look at it. You read that piece in the *Gazette*. Mr. Wolfe has never taken a murder suspect for a client if he thought there was any chance that he was guilty. He *knows* Whipple is innocent. So do I. The only way he can prove it is to get the murderer. That's all I can tell you or your conscience."

He kept trying to focus on me without blinking. "I can't stand it," he said, "and I don't intend to. An innocent man convicted of murder because I didn't have the guts . . ." He shut his eyes tight and jerked his head from side to side.

"Look," I said, "let's get down to cases. What did you lie to the police about?"

"About where I was. That evening. I lied to Wolfe too. I wasn't at the club all evening. I left right after dinner and was gone for more than two hours."

My lips parted to say "Where did you go?" but it didn't get out. I don't know what stopped it. You never know where a hunch comes from; if you did it wouldn't be a hunch. I took three seconds to look at it, liked it, and said, "Sure. You went and baby-sat for Dolly Brooke while she went and got her car and went for a ride."

It stopped the blinks. He stared. "How in the name of . . ."

I grinned at him. "You have just heard a detective detect. I knew that she had got the car from the garage around a quarter to eight and returned about an hour and a half later. I doubted if she would leave an eight-year-old alone in the apartment. You come and make a big point of not owing them any loyalty and then say you lied about where you were that evening. So I detect." I turned a palm up. "Simple. Now that the beans are spilled, let's use the broom. Where did she go in the car?"

He still wasn't blinking. "So you knew. I didn't need . . . I'm a damn fool. How did you find out?"

"Confidential information. We respect confidences, including yours. Where did—"

"Did you know when we were here? Friday?"

"No. We got it last night. Where did she go in the car?"

"I didn't need to come." He got to his feet, none too steady. "You already knew." He turned and was going.

I moved and was between him and the door. "*Now* you're a damn fool," I told him. "The only question is would you rather tell me or the police."

He was blinking again. "You said you respect confidences."

"Nuts. You know what I said. We would prefer to tell the police nothing, about you or anyone else, until we can name the murderer, but you're not leaving until either (a) you answer my questions or (b) I get a cop here and you answer *his* questions. Take your pick."

He didn't size me up. He stood and blinked at me, but not to decide if he could rush me. He was contemplating the situation, not me. I let him take his time. Finally he turned, not too sure of his legs, walked back to the chair, and sat. Back in my chair, I asked him, not demanding, just wanting to know, "Where did she go in the car?"

"If I tell you that," he said, "I ought to tell you all about it."

"Fine. Go ahead."

He took a while to decide where to start. "You know I was going to marry Susan."

"If that's the way you want to put it, yes."

"That's exactly the way I want to put it. We knew about that apartment. We all knew—her mother, Kenneth, Dolly, and I. We knew she was emotionally involved in the civil rights movement. Her mother and Dolly thought she was also emotionally involved with that man, Dunbar Whipple, but I didn't. I thought I understood Susan, and I still think so. You don't think so, do you?"

There was no point to rubbing salt in. "I don't count. I didn't know her. All I want is to get a murderer."

"Well, I knew her. I understood her. Her mother and Dolly kept saying I ought to do something, but I thought it was better just to let her work her way through it. They kept harping about that apartment and the disgrace, the scandal, Susan would bring on the family. Then about a month ago Dolly said if I wouldn't do something she would. She didn't tell Kenneth because she knew he wouldn't approve, but she told me. Some evening when Kenneth was staying at the laboratory Mother Brooke would come and stay with the boy, and she would go up there and see what was going on. In one way I didn't approve either, but in another way I did, because I thought she would find there was nothing wrong. You see the situation?"

I only nodded. *What* a situation for a grown man with a brain supposedly in working order. I wasn't thinking of color; that was an unimportant detail.

"All right," he said, "that's how it was. That evening, that Monday evening, I got a phone call as I was eating dinner at the club. It was Dolly. Mother Brooke couldn't come because she was sick, and Dolly wanted me to come and stay with the boy. I suppose I should have refused, but—anyway, I went. I got there a little after eight. She left right away, and—"

"Hold it. Our information is that she got the car from the garage about a quarter to eight."

"Then your information is wrong. She left the house about ten after, and the garage is four blocks away. My God, do you think I don't know? When I know what happened? When I've been over it and over it a thousand times?"

"Okay, you know."

"God knows I do. Give her ten minutes to get to the garage and get the car, and ten more to One Hundred and Twenty-eighth Street, and—"

"Maybe not enough. Fifteen."

"No. Straight up Park Avenue and across, nothing to it at that time in the evening. I drove it and timed it twice yesterday. Nine minutes both times, and I didn't push. So she got there just after half past eight, out of the car and to the building. She went up the two flights and stood at the door of the apartment a few minutes, listening. She didn't hear anything, and she knocked on the door and then stood some more, and then knocked again, and nothing happened. I'm telling you what she told me. She went down and stood across the street, and pretty soon Dunbar Whipple came and entered the building. She wanted—"

"Did she know Whipple?"

"She had met him. Susan had taken her to a couple of ROCC meetings. She wanted to go back in and up to the apartment, but she was afraid to. She went back to the car, which she had double-parked around the corner, and drove to the garage and came home. If you allow twenty-five minutes for that, Whipple got to the apartment at five minutes after nine. It was exactly half past when she got home."

"And told you what had happened."

"Yes."

"What was her—uh—attitude?"

"She was excited. She thought she had proved something, but I didn't. I thought obviously Susan wasn't there, since Dolly had knocked twice and she hadn't answered. A girl who works for the ROCC lived in that building, Susan had told me about her, and Whipple could have been going to see her. We got into an argument about it, and I left and went back to the club."

I regarded him. He was really a pitiful sight. "Tell me something. Just curiosity. Why were you so hot to know why we think Whipple is innocent when you already knew damn well he is?"

"I didn't *know* it."

"Certainly you did. Only two alternatives. Either Susan was already dead when Dolly arrived, since she didn't answer the door, or she did answer the door and let Dolly in, and Dolly killed her. In either case she wasn't alive at five minutes past nine. Don't tell me you hadn't figured that."

"Of course I had. But it wasn't *certain*. Sometimes people don't go to the door when there's a knock."

"Nuts. No wonder you had conscience trouble. You think Dolly killed her and you baby-sat for her while she did it."

"I haven't said so and I'm not going to." He was blinking again. If his eyelashes had been wings he would have been around the world by now. He asked, "What are you going to do?"

I looked at my watch: 10:43. "Nothing, for seventeen minutes. Mr. Wolfe comes down from the plant rooms at eleven. I would advise— Oh, a question. Did you tell her you were going to spill it?"

"No. It would have been . . . tough. She would have tried to talk me out of it."

"Are you going to tell her you *have* spilled it?"

"No."

"Good. Don't. I advise you to flop. Now that it's off your chest you can probably do twelve hours. We have an extra room with a good bed. In your condition you might get run over crossing the street."

He shook his head. "I'm going home. God, the sound of that, going home!" He got to his feet and put a hand on the chair back for help. "I don't want Wolfe to see me. I couldn't take him right now. Can't you tell me what you're going to do?"

"I have no idea. Mr. Wolfe is the cook, I only wait on table. As for your lying to the police, forget it. They expect it. If nobody ever lied to them, most of them would have been out of jobs long ago." I rose. "If it has to be that you hear from them, you'll hear from me first." I touched his arm. "Come along. Get home in one piece if possible."

The guy was just about out on his feet. After I got his coat on him, and his hat, and opened the door, I wanted to convoy him down the stoop, but if he couldn't manage that he would never make it home, so I stood out in the raw March wind and watched him to Tenth Avenue, where he would sooner or later get a taxi headed uptown. Of course the trouble was the letup after getting rid of a ten-ton load.

Even after he had reached the corner I stayed on the stoop, for the air, while I asked myself if I should have kept him for more digging. For instance, granting that Dolly had killed her, had it been planned or offhand? I might have asked him if Dolly was good at mimicking, and if he had ever heard her imitate Susan's voice, perhaps to him on the phone. Wolfe would have I might have asked him what Dolly had said when she came back, tried to get her exact words. If she had just committed a murder, smashed her sister-in-law's skull with a club, almost certainly her tongue had made some little slip, and probably more than one. I had collected four or five might-haves when a bellow came from inside.

"What are you doing out there?"

I bellowed back, "Breathing!" went in, shut the door, and followed him to the office. It was useless to try to start conversation until he had put a spray of Phalaenopsis Aphrodite in the vase and glanced through the mail. It's some kind of compulsion. I suspect that he always hopes to find a letter from a collector in Honduras or somewhere, saying that he has found a clear solid blue orchid and is sending it to Wolfe by air, no charge, to show his appreciation for something or other.

It wasn't there that morning. I open the mail. He put it aside and turned to me. "Mr. Magnus?"

"He'll be here this afternoon. Miss Kallman had it all arranged when she phoned while I was at breakfast, very much on the job, which may mean something and may not. But something more interesting; I know where Dolly Brooke went in her car that evening."

"You do."

"Yes, sir. Peter Vaughn came and we talked nearly an hour. He just left. I don't think you need it verbatim, so I'll just tell it."

I did so. Not word for word, but I covered all the points. After the first few sentences he leaned back with his chin down and closed his eyes, as he always does when all he needs is his ears. When I finished, explaining that I had let him go because I was human, as he had said, he held it for another minute and then opened his eyes.

He grunted. "You are not more human than I am. You are

merely more susceptible, more sociable, and more vulnerable."

"Just words. Shall we settle it now?"

"No. We have something more urgent to settle. Is it possible that Mr. Vaughn's account is gammon?"

"Not a chance. He's wide open. I wouldn't even name odds."

"Did that woman kill her?"

"I pass. Again no odds, for a different reason. I may understand women better than Vaughn does, I hope I do, but I pass as it stands now. The only visible motive is a little limp. If she did it to keep scandal from the family name, what about *this* scandal? Pass."

He straightened up. "Whether she did or not, we could have Mr. Whipple released from custody today. Tomorrow at the latest."

"Sure. If she sticks to the line she gave Vaughn, and she had better. She'll have to. As I told Vaughn, it's obvious that Susan wasn't in there alive when Whipple arrived. Shall I get Cramer? I promised Vaughn nothing."

He made a face. "I don't like it."

"You wouldn't. You're on record that the only way to clear Whipple is to produce the murderer, and she may not be it. We have found an out for him, but we can't be sure he would stay out. She might change the script and say she didn't enter the building, and we can't prove she did. I don't like it either."

"You just said she would have to stick to the line she gave Vaughn."

"I'm more vulnerable than you are. I talk too fast. As soon as I said it I realized it wasn't true."

He growled. "Confound it." He made fists and rested them on the edge of his desk. He looked at the left one, saw nothing helpful, looked at the right one, saw no better, and looked at me. "When can you get her here?"

"Oh, thirty minutes or thirty hours. When do you want her?"

"I don't know."

"Tell me when you do. Of course I'll have to pry her loose, and I only have one pry. On the way she'll have plenty of time to decide what line to take."

He scowled at me. I scowled back, but his face gives him the advantage. Finding that that wasn't getting us anywhere, he leaned back and closed his eyes, and his lips started working. They pushed out, then drew in, and kept at it—out and in, out and in . . . Man at work, or possibly genius at work. I never interrupt the lip act because I can't; he's not there. It may last anywhere from half a minute to half an hour; I always time it, since there's nothing else to do. That time it was four minutes. He opened his eyes and asked, "Can Saul be here at two o'clock?"

"Yes. I rang him before breakfast. He had a chore for this morning, but he'll be free around noon and will call."

"Tell him two o'clock. Get Mr. Whipple."

Everything pertaining to a current operation is kept in a locked drawer, and I had to use a key to get the extension number at the university. Then there was a wait because he was in another room. When I had him, Wolfe got on. Naturally Whipple had questions about last night's meeting, and Wolfe tolerated him as much as he would a client who was going to get a fat bill. Not more. He stopped him by saying he hadn't called to report.

"I report only when there has been progress. I called because I need your help. I need two Negroes, and I assume you have Negro friends. Two men neither too young nor too old, preferably between thirty and fifty. Not too light, the blacker the better. Not elegant in appearance; that's essential. Rather roughly dressed if possible. Average intelligence will do, or even below average; no acumen or skill is necessary. I need them here by two o'clock, or two-thirty at the latest. I don't know how long they'll have to stay, but I think not more than two hours, perhaps less. They will be asked to do nothing reprehensible or hazardous; they will take no risk of any kind. Can you supply them?"

Silence for five seconds, then: "I suppose it's something about —for my son?"

"Certainly, since I'm asking your help. There may be a development that will show promise."

"Thank God."

"He is not its source. Can you supply two such men?"

"I *will*. You'd better repeat the specifications."

Wolfe did so, but I didn't listen. I was too busy trying to guess what kind of charade was going to have two roughly dressed middle-aged Negroes in the cast. Plus, apparently, Saul Panzer.

We hung up and he turned to me. "Your notebook. On my letterhead, but not a letter. A document. Dated today. Two carbons. Double-spaced. 'I hereby affirm that at or about twenty minutes past eight in the evening of Monday, March second, nineteen sixty-four, I took my motor car from the'— name the garage and its address—'and, comma, unaccompanied, comma, drove it to One Hundred and Twenty-eighth Street in Manhattan, New York City. I parked the car, comma, walked to the entrance of the building at'—give the address—'entered the building, comma, and ascended two flights of stairs. On the third floor I . . .'"

10

At least half of the hallmen in New York apartment houses are either hard of hearing or don't give a damn. I know how to pronounce my name without mumbling, but I have heard myself announced as Godwin, Gooden, Gordon, Goodman, and variations; and with a message of five words or more they're hopeless. So that Tuesday afternoon when I entered the lobby of that sixteen-story Park Avenue palace and crossed the maybe-Oriental carpet to meet the hallman, I was prepared. I had it in my hand. Reaching him, I pointed emphatically to my mouth, shook my head, and handed it to him—a slip of paper on which I had typed:

> Please tell Mrs. Kenneth Brooke that Mr. Goodwin is here and wants to go up and tell her the answer to the question which Mr. Wolfe refused to answer last Friday evening.

He looked at me suspiciously and asked, "Deaf and dumb?" I shook my head.

"Oh, you can hear?"

I nodded.

He read it again, went through a door, used a phone, and came out. "Fourteen A," he said, and I crossed the carpet again, to the elevator. I had saved three minutes and a lot of breath.

I was admitted to Fourteen A, to a foyer bigger than my bedroom, by the lady of the house, the full-sized positive blonde. Since she was now definitely a candidate, she deserved more than mere curiosity. As I disposed of my coat and hat on a chair and followed her through an arch into a room in which a concert-size piano was merely a speck in a corner, I was trying to see a sign of a murderer in her. After all the years I should know better, and I do, but it's automatic and you can't control it.

She crossed to one of two divans at right angles to the fireplace, and when she had sat I took a nearby chair. She looked at me with her round blue eyes as a lady of that much house looks at an article like a private detective and said, "Well?"

"It was just a dodge," I said, "to get up and in."

"A *dodge*?"

"Yes. Mr. Wolfe wants to see you. You wouldn't be impressed by the reason he had for deciding that Dunbar Whipple was innocent because it was strictly personal. The same with me. Whipple was in the office for more than an hour last Tuesday, a week ago today, and from what he said and the way he said it we were convinced that he hadn't killed Susan Brooke."

She stared. "Just what he *said*?"

"Right. But now we have a better reason—maybe not actually better, but a different kind. Now we *know*. Since you stood at the door a while, listening, and heard nothing, and knocked on the door, and stood some more to listen, and knocked again, and got no response, and still heard nothing; and since when you left the building you watched the entrance, and Susan didn't arrive but Whipple did, it's obvious that she wasn't in the apartment alive when he entered. That's simple, isn't it?"

She was fairly good. She had parted her lips, and her frown was okay. But what she said wasn't so hot. She said, "What on earth do you think you're saying? Are you crazy?"

Of course people have word habits, she had asked her husband if he was crazy, but she should have done better. "That's wasted, Mrs. Brooke," I said. "Peter Vaughn couldn't handle his conscience, and we have it all from him—that is, his end of it. We have some from others too—people who saw you."

"You're crazy! What could you have from Peter Vaughn?"

I shook my head. "Really, it's no good. For his part, corroboration to burn. The hallman and elevator man who saw him come and go, and you go and come, your eight-year-old son—but it shouldn't be necessary to drag him in—the man at the garage. Peter's part is solid. It's the other part that Mr. Wolfe wants to discuss with you. I go on talking to give you time to swallow it. He wants to see you, now, and I came to escort you. The other time you wanted to see him, to find out if he knew that you had gone there that evening. Now it's his turn, he wants to see you. Let's go and get it over with."

I thought, as I talked, that she was going to go feminine on me, and so did she. She stretched an arm to put her hand out, but I wasn't close enough for her to touch me without leaving the divan. The feminine was in her eyes, and in her chin as it quivered a little, but that was all, except her saying, "I don't want to go." Pure feminine.

"Of course you don't. So come on." Masculine. I stood up.

"You said 'the other part.' What other part?"

"I'm not sure. It's what Mr. Wolfe wants to ask you about. I advise you to come and find out."

"I'm not . . . I'll come . . . later." She got to her feet, took a step, and put her hand on my arm. "Later?"

"It's already later. Whipple has been in the coop four days, and he's innocent and you know it." I took her arm and turned her, masculine but not rough, and she moved. She said she had to tell the maid and headed for a door in the rear, and I thought she might forget to come back, but no. When she returned she had a new look; she had decided to cope. If I had touched her arm I would have been cold-shouldered. But she permitted me to hold her platinum mink and to open and close the door. Down in the lobby, as the hallman opened that door for us, I told him distinctly, "You may keep that slip of paper for a souvenir," and he almost lost his grip on the door. In the taxi she wasn't talking; she kept her head turned, looking out the window. Undoubtedly she was doing what I had told Wolfe she would have time for, deciding on her line.

The charade began when we entered the hall of the old brownstone. The front door on the left, which is to the front room, was ajar half an inch, so I knew the office was empty, and Saul knew we had arrived. The whole ground floor is soundproofed, including the doors. She preferred to keep her coat, and I took her to the office, to the red leather chair, told her there would be a brief wait, left, closing the door, and proceeded to the alcove at the end of the hall. Wolfe was there by the hole in the wall with the panel opened. He looked a question, and I nodded. If there had been any important departure from the script, either at his end or mine, we would have had to go to the kitchen to discuss it.

I looked at my watch: 3:18. The wait was to be ten minutes

from the time we entered the house, at exactly a quarter past. We stood it out. At 3:24 we both got our eyes at the hole, and it was close quarters. For the twentieth time I decided that the hole must be enlarged.

It was an absolutely perfect performance. All three of them, including Saul, had arrived before two o'clock, and I had been present at the briefing, though not at the rehearsing. Simply perfect. At 3:25 the connecting door to the front room opened and they entered, Saul in the lead, and she turned her head to face them. It can't be marked against Saul that he didn't look sinister; he couldn't, with his big nose and flat ears and high sloping forehead. The first Negro was a big husky guy, as black as Cass Faison, in a blue sweater and gray slacks that hadn't been pressed since Christmas. The second one was small and wiry, not so black, in a brown suit with light tan stripes, white shirt, and red tie. Neat and clean, but not elegant.

Saul led the way across and stopped at Wolfe's desk, and they lined up there, side by side, facing Dolly Brooke in the red leather chair, ten feet away. For thirty long seconds they stood, no movement, gazing at her. She gazed back. At one point her jaw moved and I thought she was going to speak, but she didn't. Of course Saul was counting the seconds. I have timed him on it and he's never off more than one to a minute. He looked at the other two, and they both nodded. He nodded back and they filed out, not to the front room but to the hall, closing the door behind them.

I slid the panel shut, no noise, and Wolfe and I went to the kitchen. When the door had swung shut he grunted and said, "Satisfactory."

"Awful corny," I said, "and awful tough. Why she didn't

scream or throw something or jump up and run I don't know. I wish I understood women."

"Pfui. Need you report?"

"No. I followed instructions and she reacted more or less as expected. What I need after that is a drink, and I have six or seven minutes." I went to a cupboard for a bottle of Big Sandy and to a shelf for a glass, poured, and took a healthy sip. Fritz, who was at the sink sprinkling watercress, said, "There's milk in the refrigerator."

"Not when I've just watched three grown men bully a poor little woman." I took a sip.

"She is not little and she may be a murderer."

"Murderess. You mustn't call a female Jew a Jewess, and you mustn't call a female Negro a Negress, but it's okay to call a female murderer a murderess." I took a sip.

"Why?" he demanded.

"Because they resent it. That's another civil right, resenting things. I resent being called a private eye or a hawkshaw, so don't do it." I looked at my watch, took a sip, put the glass on the big table, and told Wolfe, "Time's up unless you want to stretch it."

"I don't." He moved and I followed. Saul was in the hall, up front. He had let the other members of the cast out and was standing by, to stop her if she decided to duck. Wolfe sent him a nod, which he had coming, and opened the door to the office.

Dolly Brooke turned her head, jumped up, and demanded, "Who were those men?"

He circled around her to his desk, sat, and regarded her. "Will you please be seated, madam?"

"Tricks," she said. "Tricks! Who were they?"

"When you stand I must crane. Will you sit?"

She sat down, on the edge of the chair. "Who were they?"

"I may name them later, or may not. Obviously they were identifying you as someone they had seen somewhere. It—"

"Where?"

"Let me finish a sentence. Mr. Goodwin has told you of the information furnished by Mr. Vaughn regarding his movements that Monday evening. As evidence of Mr. Whipple's innocence that information was invaluable, but it had a flaw. Faced with it, you might say that the account you gave Mr. Vaughn was an invention; that you had not entered the building; even that you had not driven there. Therefore it was necessary to establish the fact that you had entered the building and approximately the times you entered and left. That has been done. The white man was Mr. Saul Panzer, who has no peer as an investigator. The Negroes were reputable citizens who live in Harlem. For the present I withhold their names; you may learn them later, in a courtroom, if the point becomes an issue."

"Are you . . ." She let it hang. Her face had taken me along on her trip as she realized she had been flushed out of the tall grass. "You mean they saw me?"

Wolfe turned a palm up. "Could I make it any plainer, madam?"

He sure could. Me, I would have just said yes. I happen to prefer a straightforward lie to one with curves, but I admit it's a question of personal taste. It isn't that he wants to have an out; he simply likes them fancy.

She looked at me, saw only a manly truth-loving phiz, returned to Wolfe, and took a skip. "Peter Vaughn," she said with feeling. "I owe this to him." Another skip. "My husband." Still another. "Do the police know?"

"Not yet." Wolfe opened a drawer and took out a document. "I suppose they'll have to eventually, but it's barely possible that they won't. Archie?"

I arose and took the document and handed it to her and stayed on my feet, since she would soon need a pen.

"Read it," Wolfe said. "I made it as brief as possible."

She was a slow reader. I thought she would never finish the first page, and she took even longer with the second. Finally she looked up. "If you think I'm going to sign this," she said, "you're crazy."

"You won't even consider it?"

"I will not."

"Get Mr. Cramer, Archie."

"Who is Mr. Cramer?"

"A police inspector."

I was at my desk, starting to dial.

"Don't *do* that!" she yelled. I could use a nicer word, but a yell is a yell. As I went on dialing, she bounced out of the chair, to me, and grabbed my arm and jerked. She turned to Wolfe and presumably was glaring; her back was to me.

"I won't squabble," Wolfe snapped. "You will sign that statement, now, or you will stay until Mr. Cramer comes." He turned his head and roared. "Saul!"

The door opened and Saul was there. "This woman prevented Archie from making a telephone call," Wolfe told him. "Don't let her do it again."

Three men and one poor little woman. Saul advanced. I lifted the receiver, which I had cradled. "Don't," she said. She touched my arm. "Please don't. I'll sign it." The document was on the floor, where it had dropped when she bounced. Saul picked it up and handed it to her. She went to the chair and sat, and I took her a pen. The little stand beside the chair was mainly for signing checks, but it would do for signing statements too.

"All three copies," Wolfe said, and I got the two carbons from a drawer and took them to her. As she did each one I took it and gave the signature a look. It slanted up, which I understand means something, I forget what. I went to my desk and put them in the locked drawer. Saul went over to a chair by the bookshelves.

Dolly Brooke said, begging, not telling, "My husband mustn't know. The police mustn't know."

Wolfe eyed her. "It's thorny," he said. "With that statement I could get Mr. Whipple released from custody, but to clear him conclusively I must expose the murderer. The statement would be more to the point if it said that when you knocked at the door Miss Brooke admitted you, and you killed her."

She goggled. "Are you crazy?"

"No. Did you? Kill her?"

"No!"

"I hope not. If you did, as long as I reserve that statement I'll be withholding vital evidence; and I prefer to reserve it, tentatively. You say the police mustn't know. On the contrary, they probably must, sooner or later; but I would like to postpone it until I can name the murderer, and it's possible that by then your movements that evening will be of no consequence. I have—"

"You won't tell them?"

"Not immediately. I have a question that is of consequence. I want you to concentrate on it all your powers of observation and memory. If you didn't kill her, the person who did left the apartment and building within minutes, perhaps seconds, of the time you arrived. Possibly *as* you arrived. He may have been in the third-floor hall, leaving, as you mounted the stairs, and retreated to the floor above, remained there until you departed, and left the building soon after you. Or, bolder or stupider, he may have passed you on the stairs, descending as you mounted. Search your memory. Whom did you see, either while you were in the building, or leaving it after you did, as you stood and watched the entrance?"

"I didn't see anybody."

"No one at all?"

"Yes. No one in the building or leaving it."

Wolfe's head turned. "What about it, Archie?"

"Possible," I said. "Granting that she didn't enter the apartment, that she stayed in the hall, it was only about twenty minutes. It was between eight-thirty and nine, when people are set for the evening, at the movies or at home or somewhere. It's quite possible."

"Pfui." He had looked at the clock a couple of times, and he looked again. Two minutes to four. He pushed his chair back, rose, and scowled down at her. "You're in a pickle, madam. If you killed her, you're doomed. If you didn't, your chance of escaping a painful and perilous ordeal depends wholly on my competence and wit and luck." He headed for the door, but a step short of it he stopped and wheeled to say, "And Mr. Goodwin's." He turned and went. The sound of the elevator came.

She was looking at me, and from her eyes it seemed likely that she was deciding to go feminine again. Her mouth opened and closed. Finally she said, "You're Mr. Goodman."

I said, "Are you crazy?"

She stared.

"Look," I said, "if the best you can do is to tell me what my name is and get it wrong, you may not be crazy but you're pooped. There's absolutely nothing you can do except sign off and stay off." I stood up. "Since I brought you, I suppose I should take you home, but I'm expecting a caller. I'll see you to a taxi." I moved, toward the door, and she got up and came. Saul gave me a wink as I passed. It's his one bad habit.

11

Like everyone else, including you, I frequently make assumptions on insufficient grounds. All I knew about William Magnus was what Rae Kallman had told me, that he was a student at the NYU law school in Washington Square, and that he had arranged a meeting for Susan Brooke to plug civil rights and the ROCC. So I knew what he would be like: earnest and honest, of course, and dedicated; probably underfed, but the fire of freedom in his eyes; either a sweater and unpressed pants, or, if he knew the importance of correct appearance, an almost-clean white shirt and gray tie and a dark gray suit, a little worn but without a spot. Perhaps I should mention that I wouldn't be caught dead in a white shirt except when an evening requires the uniform.

Therefore when the doorbell rang a little before five o'clock and I went to the hall and saw a handsome halfback in a two-hundred-dollar camel's hair coat, of course it wasn't Magnus.

But it was. I went and opened the door. His handshake was firm and friendly, but not dedicated. His voice was full and friendly, but not pushy. When I turned from hanging the coat up, I saw as much of a custom-made blue-and-yellow-checked shirt as a two-button brown tweed jacket would let me see. When I took him to the office he flopped into the red leather chair as if it belonged to him. That made it complicated, because at my desk I would be twelve feet away, so I went and took Wolfe's chair, and he grinned and said, "You don't belong there, do you?"

I gave him the grin back. "I always belong wherever I am."

He frowned. "Who said that?"

"I did."

"No, really. You read that somewhere."

"Nope. You fed me a slider and I just happened to connect."

He grinned. "Okay, you're on base. Shall I try to pick you off?"

"I might steal on you. Let me toss one. Did Susan Brooke make a phone call at a quarter past five on Monday, March second?"

He leaned back and crossed his legs. His dark brown socks, with light brown stripes, had set him, or his old man, back four bucks. "The trouble is," he said, "that when I am asked questions I get an irresistible itch to give trick answers. It's probably a neurosis. You'd better just let me tell it. The cop that tried me first, and the lawyer—what's his name, wait a minute, Oster, that's it—and the assistant district attorney, they all insisted on asking questions, and I'm afraid they got somewhat confused. I don't want to confuse you too. I wish you'd tell me who said that about always belonging wherever you are. Or wrote it."

"Damn it, *I* did. If anyone beat me to it, I don't know who or when or where. Tell me about Susan Brooke and the phone call."

"Sure. I'm enjoying this. Nero Wolfe's office." He looked around. "That's the biggest globe I ever saw. Nice rug. Books and books. I'd love to spend a week going through all those files. It would probably teach me more than a year at law school. Anyway, I'm going into politics. I'm going to be governor of New York." Having uncrossed his legs to look around, he crossed them again. "But you want to hear about Susan Brooke."

"That was the idea."

"Did you know her?"

"No. I met her once. Five days before she died."

"I met her a year ago. She was a lovely little dame, but I'm going to wait until I'm thirty to marry. It was on account of her I got onto civil rights. I wanted to help her, and anyway, if you're in politics you're in civil rights whether you like it or not. I set up that meeting for her that day. I am now telling you."

He uncrossed his legs, and his face changed completely. He was working. "It was in a room across the hall from an office used by members of the faculty. There's a phone in the office, extension seven-nine-three, and I had arranged to use it from four-thirty on and pay for the calls. I'm disposing of that factor. Twelve local calls were made on that phone between four-thirty and six-thirty, and I made three of them. Two of my calls were to the ROCC, but neither of them was anywhere near a quarter past five. No record was kept at the switchboard of the numbers called or the exact times. Is that covered?"

"Trick answer. Yes."

"I expected about forty people, and at five o'clock about

forty were there, students and three or four faculty members. Only a few were seated. It's a big room, and we were moving around, groups here and there. I didn't call the meeting to order until Susan came, and she was late. I don't know exactly what time she arrived, and apparently no one does. I was over by a window, talking with four or five students, and she came and said, 'Here I am, late as usual.' I looked at my watch. Twenty minutes past five. So there it is. To my knowledge, it's possible that she had used the phone across the hall, but did she? I don't know. I have asked around, and I haven't found anyone who does know. Questions."

"I wouldn't dream of asking a question. If I did, it wouldn't be about the phone call; you've wrapped that up. It would be about how long the meeting lasted and when did Susan leave and so on."

He grinned. "You know how to handle me. If you go into politics, you can be senator and I'll be governor. The meeting adjourned at six-thirty, but a few of us stuck around a little while. Susan and I left at six-forty. My car was in a nearby garage, and I drove her home. By 'home' I mean the address on Park Avenue where she lives with her mother. I didn't know about the apartment in Harlem. Of course I do now. Everybody does. To finish, we arrived a little after seven, say ten after. That, as they put it in questions, was the last time I saw her alive. Alive or dead. Why did Nero Wolfe decide that Whipple didn't kill her?"

I grinned. "You're inviting it."

"Sure. Let's hear it."

"Because he knows *you* did."

He shook his head. "That's not very good. Try another. What was my motive?"

"You thought she was pregnant, thanks to you, and it would louse up your political career."

"That's a little better. Why wasn't I seen? My superb physique, my noble countenance, why wasn't I noticed there in the middle of Harlem?"

"Burnt cork."

He threw his head back and laughed. "Wonderful! You're all right. You be governor and I'll be senator. Does Nero Wolfe think he knows who killed her?"

Wolfe wouldn't be down from the plant rooms for nearly an hour, so I permitted him to stay and enjoy himself a while longer. Also he was now a candidate, though at the bottom of the list, since he had called Susan a lovely dame and implied that he might have married her if he hadn't had other ideas. Since he was deliberately planning to go into the roughest game on earth, politics, nothing was beyond or beneath him, even clubbing a lovely dame, if he had a good enough reason.

When he had gone I got busy at the typewriter. Wolfe had told Dolly Brooke that it was possible that the police would never know about her trip to Harlem, but it looked to me like very long odds, and it wouldn't hurt to have a record, made while it was fresh, of what had been said, both at her apartment and in the office. If withholding evidence got to be an issue, I would be in it as deep as he was. In the Bastille I would have plenty of time to write my memoirs, and it would be helpful to have notes if I could smuggle them in. I was banging away and had got to where Wolfe said, 'I made it as brief as possible,' by six o'clock, when he came. He went to his desk and sat, and didn't pick up his book, so I swiveled to face him.

"Mr. Magnus?" he asked.

I nodded. "It's too bad you missed him. I don't know what he would be worth stripped, but fully dressed he represents an outlay of about a grand. He's big and beaming and very chatty, but he can report almost as well as I can. Like this."

I told it, omitting all the mere chatter except the questions to which I had given trick answers. Wolfe's frown got deeper as I went along.

"So," I finished, "in a week of plugging you might find that she made the phone call, but probably you could never prove that she didn't. Oster was right when he said you wouldn't get anything conclusive. It could be that Magnus was in the office across the hall when she came, and heard her make the call, and knew that Whipple wouldn't be there until nine o'clock, and drove her there and killed her, but I doubt it. His skull is not empty. It would be a cinch to check on where he was at a quarter past five."

"She didn't make the call."

"Yeah, I know. You have two ways of deciding things. One, on the strength of evidence and deduction. Two, on the strength of genius and to hell with deduction. Which in this case means to hell with Maud Jordan."

"She was committed. She had signed a statement. Hadn't she?"

"Sure. To get away from the DA's office without signing a statement you have to thumb your nose. She would sign."

"It would be convenient to know if Mrs. Brooke has shown talent as a mimic. Mr. Vaughn could have told you this morning."

"I knew that would be mentioned sooner or later. He could barely walk. Right now he's pounding his ear. Is it urgent?"

"No." His eyes were narrowed at me. "I presume you're aware of the situation."

"I am. First, if Dolly Brooke killed her we had better prove it quick or turn that document over to Cramer. That document is hot. But we can't possibly prove it. We've got her at the door, but we can't get her inside unless we dig up a motive with legs. Do we put Saul and Fred and Orrie on that for a month or so?"

He made a face. "No."

"Second, Beth Tiger, and on her I must get personal. I have some idea, from things you've said these two weeks, how you feel about a colored man marrying a white girl. You don't feel. How about a white man marrying a colored girl?"

"Pfui."

"You may have a surprise coming. So far it may be only lust, but as I ate breakfast this morning I caught myself wondering if she can make Creole fritters, and you know what that may mean—or I suppose you don't. My room would do for both of us for a while, until the little ones start to come, and as for their color of course I can't say. As for the professional situation, she too was in the building, and she had a much better motive than Mrs. Brooke; she wanted to marry Dunbar herself."

"Presumably."

"Not presumably, certainly. That will be a problem for me, but I'll manage. Professionally, the problem is to get her down one flight and into the apartment. Have you any suggestions?"

"No."

"Neither have I. If Mrs. Brooke and Miss Tiger are filed, it could have been someone else who lives in the building. Saul and Fred and Orrie could check on all the tenants in a few days, and if they drew a blank we would know that the murderer probably entered the building around eight o'clock or soon after, and left it before Mrs. Brooke arrived. Someone in the neighborhood probably saw him coming or going. Saul and

Fred and Orrie would be handicapped for that combing job by their color, so it would be better to use three or four Negro operatives. There are quite a few available. Okay?"

"No."

"I agree. That was third. Fourth, have Saul and Fred and Orrie check the alibis of the ROCC staff. Not just the ones who were here, all thirty-four of them. Some of them may have felt as Ewing did about Dunbar marrying a white girl, only more so. Any of them *might* have known about the phone call. One of the females might have been able to imitate Susan's voice, and she might have left at five o'clock. But the main thing, check all their alibis. Three weeks should do it, or maybe four. Does that appeal to you?"

"No."

"Very well. You presumed that I am aware of the situation and I said I am. There isn't one single solitary sensible thing that you can do or I can do or Saul and Fred and Orrie can do."

He nodded. "You're right." He switched the reading light on and picked up the book he was just starting, *Science: The Glorious Entertainment,* by Jacques Barzun.

I glared at him. He had made a monkey of me. One of my main functions, perhaps the mainest, is to ride him if and when he lies down on the job, and he had muzzled me. My intention, of course, had been to dare him to suggest a move, to show how much smarter he was than me, and he knew it.

"Go to hell," I said emphatically and turned to the typewriter and banged.

I don't know how long he would have stalled on that one— a day or a week or forever. At dinner he started on automation. He has always been anti-machine, and on automation his position was that it would soon make life an absurdity. It was already bad enough; on a cold and windy March day he was eating his evening meal in comfortable warmth, and he had no personal connection whatever with the production of the warmth. The check that paid the oil bill was connected, but *he* wasn't. Soon, with automation, no one would have any connection with the processes and phenomena that make it possible to stay alive. We would all be parasites, living not on some other living organisms but on machines, arrived at the ultimate ignominy. I tried to put up a stiff argument, but he knows more words. We were still at it when we got up to cross to the office for coffee, and were in the hall when the doorbell rang.

It was Paul Whipple. Wolfe, seeing him through the one-way glass, let out a growl; he hadn't finished with automation. But it was the client, and besides, since we had no notion of what to do next, we had better see if he had.

No. All he had was a question. Being polite, he didn't ask it until Fritz had brought the coffee, and Wolfe had poured and I had passed, and he had taken a couple of sips. The steam dimmed his black-rimmed cheaters, and he got out a handkerchief to wipe them.

"My two friends told me what happened," he said. "They said you didn't tell them not to."

Wolfe was trying to look as if he didn't mind having unexpected company and not succeeding. "I told them they could tell you but no one else."

"They won't. You said there might be a development that would show promise. Did it?"

"Yes and no." Wolfe drank, put his cup down, and took a deep breath. "Mr. Whipple. I intended to reserve this, and if you had telephoned I would have. But you troubled to come, and you have a right to your question. Your son could be out tomorrow. Perhaps on bail, but at liberty."

The cheaters dropped to the floor, but the rug is soft. "My

God," he said, just loud enough to hear. "I knew it. I knew you could do it."

"I haven't done much. I won't give you the particulars; I'll only tell you that I have verifiable information which makes it highly unlikely that Susan Brooke was alive when your son arrived at the apartment. It is sufficiently persuasive to convince the police that it would be inadvisable to hold your son on a murder charge. But it doesn't give the murderer's name or even hint at it."

Whipple was staring, concentrating. Without his glasses he looked older. "But I don't— If she was dead when he got there . . ."

"Yes. The information makes that conclusion hard to challenge. I can have him released, probably under bail as a material witness. Then the police will be galled. They will suspect you and your wife, and everyone associated with the Rights of Citizens Committee. They will suspect your son, not of actually doing the deed but of being implicated. He can be conclusively cleared only by producing the murderer, and that will be much more difficult with the police everywhere, harassing everyone, including me. Especially me. I don't want to give them the information I have. I want them to keep your son in custody, satisfied that they have the culprit. You can of course make that impossible. You can tell me that if I withhold the information you'll tell them I have it. If you do, I'll have to give it to them at once and quit. Have I made it clear?"

"Yes." Whipple lowered his head. I had seen many people, sitting in that chair, lower or turn their heads when they found how hard it was to use their brains while they were meeting Wolfe's eyes. Seeing the glasses on the floor, he bent over to pick them up, got his handkerchief out again, and rubbed, slow motion.

"I won't urge you," Wolfe said.

He looked up. "Oh, you don't have to. I was thinking about my wife. If she knew he could be home tomorrow—but she doesn't have to know." He jerked his shoulders up. "I won't tell her." He put the glasses on. "The information—will it keep? Can you still use it, if . . ."

"I can use it at any time. I have it in writing, a signed statement, by the woman your friends saw here this afternoon."

"Will they be involved?"

"No."

"Do I know her?"

"I doubt it. I won't name her."

"I—I'm going to ask a question."

"You have already asked three. I may answer it."

"Do you know—I mean do you think you know—who killed her?"

"No. I have no inkling. I have no plan. I have only a commitment, and I intend to meet it, though at the moment I have no idea when or how. How many times has the answer to some bothersome question come while you were brushing your teeth?"

"More than once."

"I'll be brushing mine in a couple of hours. Not with an electric thing; with that machine the fear of electrocution would squelch all mental processes. As an anthropologist, are you concerned with the menace of automation?"

"As an anthropologist, no."

"As a man you are."

"Why . . . yes."

"Your son is twenty-one years old. Are you aware that by averting this calamity for him we will be compelling him inevitably to suffer a worse one?"

Very neat. Confronted by a father worried sick about a son locked up for the big one, he had dealt with that in less than a quarter of an hour and steered him to automation; a fresh audience, better than me, since he had had me at dinner. Neat.

12

I should have known better. As I sat at my breakfast table in the kitchen Wednesday morning, disposing of corn muffins and shirred eggs with sherry and chives, my eyes were on the *Times* propped on the rack, but they were sharing attention with my ears. If the house phone buzzed it would be Wolfe, in his room, to tell me to come up for instructions. I should have known better. His line about getting answers to questions while brushing his teeth had been merely a way to sneak up on automation. I don't say he has never got an idea while brushing his teeth, but if so it was when we were on something urgent. There was nothing urgent about this. What the hell, Dunbar Whipple was safe and sound, getting three meals a day—though it would have been different if Wolfe had been eating the meals. That *would* have been urgent.

That Wednesday was about as unsatisfactory a day as I have ever spent, speaking professionally. Wolfe's taking time out from a job was nothing new, far from it, but always before I had had the satisfaction of poking him; as I said, that was one of my main functions. Now I couldn't. I was on record that nobody could do anything, and that day nobody did, for sure. The only action performed or word spoken that had anything to do with the case came around five o'clock when Wolfe was up in the plant rooms fiddling with the orchids. The phone rang, and I said aloud, "Automation again." I lifted the receiver.

"Nero Wolfe's office, Archie Goodwin speaking."

"This is Peter Vaughn. I'm calling now because I knew Wolfe wouldn't be there. I can't take him."

"Neither can I. Today. Are you up and dressed?"

"Sure. I slept *seventeen hours*. I wanted to know, have you seen her?"

"Yes, and so has Mr. Wolfe. She spent an hour here yesterday afternoon. Relax. She admits it as you told it. Naturally you want to know if we have passed it on. We haven't. For the present we're saving it. I wouldn't advise you to drop in on her for tea. She'd probably put vinegar in it, or something worse. By the way, I meant to ask you yesterday, have you ever heard her do imitations? People's voices?"

"Yes, often. She's good at it. She was on the stage, you know."

"Oh, she was?"

"Yes, Dolly Drake. Not a star, nothing like that. I believe she quit when she married Kenneth, but of course I didn't know them then. Why? Why do you ask?"

"Just checking a little point. Routine. I suppose she could do Susan's voice, for instance."

"Certainly, I've heard her. I've heard her do Susan making a speech on civil rights. Naturally I didn't like it, but she's good. Listen, something I wasn't going to mention, but I guess I will.

I may have something important to tell you a little later. Can I get you there this evening?"

"Yes, but I'm here now. Shoot."

"Well, I— No, I won't. I wouldn't want to— No. Maybe I just imagined it, but I'm going to find out. I may ring you this evening."

"How are you going to find out?"

"Oh, ask a few questions. I wish I hadn't mentioned it. It's probably nothing. I want to say I'm damned grateful to you and Wolfe, not telling the police. I was pretty sure you hadn't; they would have been at me. I'm *damned* grateful."

He hung up, and I was grateful to him. He had given me something to nibble at. Was there any chance he was going to produce an item we could work on, and if so, what would it be? It would have to be about Dolly Brooke, since she and Kenneth were his only connection, but it wouldn't be about the item he had just supplied, that Dolly could imitate Susan's voice, since he had asked why I asked. Yet it might. He might have asked why I asked to see if I knew something he knew or suspected. I should have hung on. I rang him. First Heron Manhattan; he hadn't been in today. Then his home; he had just gone out and they didn't know where.

When Wolfe came down from the plant rooms I reported. He listened with his eyes open, showing that he was hearing nothing that called for concentration. It was obvious that he had decided, for some reason too subtle for me to appreciate, possibly because he didn't want to see her again if he could avoid it, that Dolly Brooke wasn't it. When I suggested that it wouldn't hurt to try to find Vaughn and pry it out of him, he said pfui, Mr. Vaughn was manifestly an ass, since he hadn't even had enough gumption to slough his illusion about Miss Brooke. That was a fitting end to the day. I had enough gumption to go up to my room, ring Lucy Valdon, and invite her to dine at Rusterman's. She suggested that we eat at her house instead. Sometimes that suggestion is welcome, and it was then. It was nice and quiet there and we could laugh louder and longer. I certainly needed someone to laugh with. If Vaughn phoned, Wolfe could tell him where to get me. I stripped and got under the shower.

My morning fog begins to let little streaks of light through as I sip orange juice, and with my second cup of coffee it's all clear, so when I go to the office around nine-thirty I'm set for the day. But there are exceptions, and that Thursday morning was one. First, it was ten-thirty instead of nine-thirty. Second, I had got home at three o'clock and had had two hours' less sleep than my regulation eight. Third, there was nothing to be set for. If there had been any word from Peter Vaughn it hadn't been worth mentioning, since there had been no note on my desk when I got home. Evidently it was going to be more of the same. I had a notion to go up and get Wolfe's toothbrush and put it on his desk, on top of the mail, but that would only make it worse. I would go for a walk and not be there when he came down. That appealed to me. My watch said 10:52. I went to the kitchen and told Fritz, and to the rack in the hall for my coat, and as I was reaching for it some object dimmed the light from the glass in the door, and I turned. The object was Inspector Cramer. Good. Anything and anybody was welcome, even him, even if he had somehow learned about Dolly Brooke and intended to take us for obstructing justice. I opened the door as he started his hand for the button, and said, "Greetings. I was standing here waiting for you."

No comment. He was not only out of sorts, he was out of

words. He took his coat off and put it on the bench, dropped his hat on it, marched to the office, looked at his watch, and stood facing the door to the hall. Going to my desk, I had a splendid view of his broad burly shoulders and his king-size fanny, motionless for a good three minutes until Wolfe entered, stopped two steps in, and glared. Cramer wheeled and went to the red leather chair. Wolfe switched the glare to me, and as he went to his desk I said, "There wasn't time to buzz you, he just came." He put a raceme of Vanda suavis in the vase, sat, and started looking through the mail, no hurry.

"Take your time," Cramer said, icy. "Take *my* time. We've got all day. You're going to tell me every word anyone has said in this room, including you and Goodwin, about the murder of Susan Brooke. Start with Peter Vaughn. How often has he been here, and when, and what was said?"

So it *was* Dolly Brooke. Her statement, all three copies, was in the safe. A safe is safer than a locked drawer.

Wolfe pushed the mail aside and swiveled. "This is extraordinary," he said, not a protest, merely an observation. "You have your murderer in custody. I have been, and am, acting in his interest as instructed by his legal attorney. Surely you don't expect to get evidence that will help convict him from *me*. Even if I had any I should not and would not disclose it to *you*. Extraordinary. Could I be wrong about the legal position? Shall I get Mr. Oster here?"

It sounded impressive, but Cramer wasn't impressed. "I know the legal position," he said, still icy. "You're not acting for Peter Vaughn, and Oster isn't his attorney. I want to know when and where you and Goodwin have seen Vaughn and what was said."

Wolfe shook his head. "Nonsense. You're rattled, and that's

extraordinary too. We have seen Mr. Vaughn only in our capacity as agents for Mr. Whipple and his lawyer, and you are here in your capacity as Mr. Whipple's legal nemesis."

"No."

Wolfe's brows went up. "No?"

"I'm here in my capacity as the head of Homicide South, but not about the murder of Susan Brooke. About the murder of Peter Vaughn."

If he was after an effect he got it. My head jerked left, to Wolfe, and his jerked right, to me. From his look at me it might have been deduced that he thought I had killed Vaughn, and from my look at him it might have been deduced that I thought he had, so Cramer must have been confused.

Wolfe's head turned back. "I presume this isn't flummery; that would be fatuous. The particulars?"

"About three hours ago a passer-by looked in the window of a parked car on Second Avenue near Thirty-second Street and told a patrolman what he had seen, and the patrolman went to look. The body of a man was on the floor in front, doubled up, the head and shoulders shoved down to the floor. He had been shot on the right side, four inches below the armpit, one shot that went between his ribs and got his heart. If death had been quick, as it almost certainly had, the shot had been fired between nine o'clock and midnight. The body has been identified. Peter Vaughn. The car is the property of his father's firm, Heron Manhattan, Inc. No weapon found. Yes, I know the legal position."

I thought, Now he'll never have to answer for lying to the police. I thought that, because at the moment there was no other thought worth thinking.

Wolfe's eyes had closed. They opened. "And Dunbar Whipple was in custody from nine o'clock to midnight?"

"You know damn well he was."

"When will he be released?"

"Nuts."

Wolfe nodded. "It's embarrassing, certainly. You know the annals of homicide. It's conceivable that another hand killed Peter Vaughn; it's even conceivable that there was no connection between his death and Susan Brooke's; but you don't believe it, and neither do I. You don't dare hold him. Confound it. This will make—"

Cramer smacked the chair arm. "Damn it, don't sit there and smirk at me! Talk! When did you last see Vaughn?"

"You don't mean 'smirk.' I am not doing what you think 'smirk' means. I'm reacting not to your discomfiture but to my own vexation. Now you need a murderer, but so do I. Coming here with a startling piece of news and barking at me is futile, and you know it." He leaned back, shut his eyes, and tightened his lips.

Cramer sat and regarded him and breathed.

Wolfe straightened up and cocked his head. "Mr. Cramer. I have no information for you. Don't explode; let me explain. We—I am including Mr. Goodwin—have seen and spoken with Mr. Vaughn twice. Last Friday evening he was here for less than an hour with Mr. and Mrs. Kenneth Brooke. None of them gave us any information that you did not already have. Day before yesterday, Tuesday morning, he came alone and spoke with Mr. Goodwin, again for less than an hour. I wasn't present, but Mr. Goodwin has reported to me. Mr. Vaughn had disclosed certain facts you don't know about, but it is my considered opinion that they have no bearing on his death. There are—"

"That's for me to say."

"It is not. There are two points. First, in our talks with Mr.

Vaughn, Mr. Goodwin and I were the agents of Mr. Oster, and therefore the communications were privileged. Second, even if they weren't privileged we would reserve them, because we have reason to believe that they have no connection with his death. If the event should prove us wrong we would of course be called to account. However—"

"I'm calling you to account here and now."

"Pfui. You know you can't. However, we'll give you one bit of information, privileged or not, which probably *is* connected with his death. He called on the telephone shortly after five o'clock yesterday and spoke with Mr. Goodwin. Archie, the possibly relevant portion of the conversation, beginning with his saying that he might have something to tell you later."

I told it, to Cramer. "He said, 'Listen, something I wasn't going to mention, but I guess I will. I may have something important to tell you a little later. Can I get you there this evening?' I said, 'Yes, but I'm here now. Shoot.' He said, 'Well, I— No, I won't. I wouldn't want to— No. Maybe I just imagined it, but I'm going to find out. I may ring you this evening.' I said, 'How are you going to find out?' He said, 'Oh, ask a few questions. I wish I hadn't mentioned it. It's probably nothing.'"

"Who was he—"

"No," Wolfe snapped. "Mr. Goodwin is *my* agent. Archie, did he give you any hint of whom he was going to question or about what?"

"No."

"Have you any notion about it?"

It was obvious he wanted another no, so I supplied it. He turned to Cramer. "Nor have I; but I suspect that his contemplated action led to his death, and so we report the conversation. If you can learn whom he expected to question before I do, you'll get the murderer."

"Damn you," Cramer said, icy again. "*Damn* you. You already know."

"I do not. I haven't even a conjecture. I have some information you don't have, but I am convinced that it has no bearing on the identity of the murderer. I have no conjecture on that either. That was our last word from Mr. Vaughn; he didn't call again. Before, I had an advantage: you thought Dunbar Whipple was the culprit, and I didn't. Now I have no advantage whatever. We're up the same stump."

"You don't say your word of honor."

"I use that phrase only when I must, to satisfy you. This time I wouldn't crook a finger to satisfy you. I wish you would leave. I need to discuss the situation with Mr. Goodwin."

"Go right ahead. I won't interrupt."

"Indeed you won't. What effect do you think automation will have on Homo sapiens?"

"Go to hell," Cramer said and got up and walked out. I went to the door but didn't stick my head into the hall until the front door slammed, and then only to see that he was outside. I returned to my desk, sat, and said, "All right, discuss."

He said, "Ggrrrrhh."

"Then I'll discuss. You told him that what Vaughn told me Tuesday had no bearing on his death. You got me to say that I had no notion about whom Vaughn was going to question or what about, when you know darned well I had. Yesterday you weren't interested in what Vaughn told me on the phone, that Mrs. Brooke could imitate Susan's voice. If it turns out that she killed Susan *and* Vaughn how will you react to *my* discomfiture?"

"I have assumed she didn't."

"I know you have. I haven't. There has been no sign whatever that Vaughn ever had any contact with anyone involved,

except the Brookes. Who else could he possibly have been
going to ask a few questions?"

"I don't know. But as for Mrs. Brooke, in addition to the
lack of acceptable motive, she couldn't have made that telephone call, mimicking Miss Brooke, unless she knew of the
eight-o'clock rendezvous, and that's unlikely; and if she didn't
make the call, who did? Possibly, of course, Miss Brooke; but
by no means certainly; I still question it. But the chief point
about Mrs. Brooke: returning home, she told Mr. Vaughn that
she had seen Mr. Whipple entering the building. Consider it.
She is in the apartment, having wiped her fingerprints from
the club with which she has just killed her sister-in-law; any
idiot would do that. She scoots; any idiot would do that too.
Outside, on the street, does she stand there until she sees Mr.
Whipple arrive and enter? Nonsense. Then does she catch a
glimpse of him, arriving, as she flees? Possibly; but if so, would
she tell Mr. Vaughn that she saw him arrive? I don't believe it."

I looked at it for five seconds. "What else?"

"Nothing ponderable."

"Okay." I stood up. "I'm taking a leave of absence without
pay. Two hours or two days, I don't know."

He nodded. "With luck it will be two hours. Your time
would be better spent on Mr. Vaughn, even with Mr. Cramer's
legion underfoot." He reached for the little stack of mail.

I blew.

I never, in these reports, skimp any step that counts, forward or backward. If I score a point, or if I get my nose pushed
in, I like to cover it. But it would be a waste of time and space
to tell you, for instance, how the Park Avenue hallman reacted
to the fact that this time I could talk, or how Dolly Brooke
took the news, news to her, that Peter Vaughn was dead.

What matters is that it wasn't a step in either direction, except for me personally, since Wolfe had already crossed her off. In less than two hours I got the kind of alibi you do get sometimes, the kind you file under finished business. At seven-forty Wednesday evening Kenneth and Dolly Brooke had sat down to dinner at the table of another couple in the same apartment house; a little before nine two other couples had joined them for an evening of bridge; and they had quit around one o'clock. I checked it with all three of the women, two in person and one on the phone, and with two of the men. When I got back to the old brownstone, Wolfe was in the dining room, halfway through lunch, and one glance at my face told him how it stood. I took my seat, and Fritz came, and I helped myself to a healthy portion of broiled shad that had been marinated in oil and lemon juice seasoned with bay leaf, thyme, and oregano, and three ladles of puréed sorrel. I took only three ladles because at bedtime I would go to the kitchen, heat the leftover sorrel, spread it on a couple of slices of Fritz's bread, and sprinkle it with nutmeg. Serve with a glass of milk. Have a spoon handy to salvage the purée that dribbles onto the plate when you bite.

When we went to the office neither of us mentioned Dolly Brooke. I merely said, as I sat, "I'll deduct twenty-two dollars for the two hours."

He grunted. "I prefer not to share the cost of this performance. I'm paying a debt." He flipped a hand to dismiss it. "Presumably Mr. Vaughn telephoned from his home."

"Only presumably. When I rang his home about half an hour later I was told he had just gone out, by a maid, on a guess."

"Where does he live?"

"East Seventy-seventh Street, between Fifth and Madison. Presumably with his parents; it's listed as Mrs. Samuel Vaughn."

"We need to know his movements yesterday, both before and after he telephoned."

"We sure do."

"How do you propose to proceed?"

"Ask people questions. Routine. If you want to speed it up at a price, Saul and Fred and Orrie could help. One advantage, everybody would have the answers ready because they would already have told the cops."

He growled. "Intolerable."

"Yes, sir. The dust would make it harder. It might be better if we just sat here and tried to guess who, or at least what kind of who, Vaughn was going to ask questions of. I had a try at it in the taxi on the way home."

"And?"

"The shape he was in when he left here Tuesday morning, he must have gone straight home and flopped. He was surely flat by one o'clock. He told me on the phone he had slept seventeen hours, and that has him awake at six a.m., so he had all day, and unquestionably he had seen somebody before he phoned me. He said he might have something important to tell me a little later. He wouldn't have said that, especially the 'important,' if he merely had some wild idea. He was going to follow up something he had seen or heard. Satisfactory?"

"Yes, but you haven't moved."

"I move now. What or who is the point. What would be eating him when he caught up on sleep? He had got Dolly Brooke off his conscience, and now two questions were nagging him: who killed Susan, and had she been emotionally involved—his words—with Dunbar Whipple, or hadn't she? As for who killed her, he thought it possible, maybe probable, that Dolly Brooke had, but that was merely an unanswered question that other people were working on. It was the second question that really hurt, and he wanted to know."

I gestured. "All right, where would he go? In a way he was a simple, direct kind of guy, and he might have gone straight to Dunbar Whipple, but he was in the can. There was no point in going to Dolly Brooke; he had heard all she had to say, he knew she didn't really know, whether she had killed Susan or not. There were only two possibilities, as far as he knew: Whipple's father and mother, or the people at the ROCC. That's where he went. To Paul Whipple, or the ROCC, or both. I suggest that you phone Whipple, and if you get a no, I go to the ROCC and ask Maud Jordan what time Peter Vaughn got there yesterday."

Wolfe's shoulders went up an eighth of an inch and down again. "It can do no harm. Even if—"

The doorbell rang. I went to the hall for a look, turned my head to tell Wolfe, "Whipple," and proceeded to the front. It was a pleasant walk, those dozen steps; I was absolutely certain that I had more than made up for the two hours I had wasted on Dolly Brooke. What else could have brought Whipple in the middle of a working day? When I opened the door and offered a hand I'm afraid I overdid it a little. I am not a knuckle-crusher, but I do have a grip, and I guess he felt it. I took him to the office, and I hope I wasn't smirking as he took the red leather chair and told Wolfe he had come instead of phoning because he had to tell him something that might make trouble for people that they didn't deserve. Wolfe asked what people, and Whipple raised a hand to adjust his glasses. Cheaters are useful that way; they give you an excuse for moving your eyes and taking a few seconds to pick words.

"You may not know," Whipple said. "That young man, Peter Vaughn, has been murdered."

Wolfe nodded. "I do know."

"His body was found in a parked car. He was shot."

"Yes."

"Well, you know—" It came out husky, and he cleared his throat and started over. "You know that in all this trouble I have been absolutely candid with you."

"I have no reason to doubt it."

"I have been. Absolutely candid. I have told you everything that you might need to know. Now there's something that I don't want to tell you, but I know I must. It will make trouble for people who are friends of mine—not only friends, they are important people in the—to my race. But to ask your help, and accept it, and then keep facts from you that you should know—that would be contemptible."

"You could tell me to quit."

"I don't want you to quit!" His voice rose, almost a shriek, and he clamped his teeth on his lip. In a moment he went on. "You'll have to make allowances. When I first came to you my nerves were none too good, and now I can't control them." His head jerked up. "This is childish. Yesterday he came to me, Peter Vaughn, and asked me to tell him what I knew of the relations that existed between my son and that girl, Susan Brooke. He wasn't—"

"What time yesterday?"

"In the morning. He was at the college waiting when I arrived. He wasn't very intelligent, was he? I told him I knew nothing about it beyond the fact of their association in their work, that I could neither confirm nor deny any of the things that have been printed. What else could I say? He was insistent, but so was I, and he left. Then during the lunch hour I received a phone call from Tom Henchy of the ROCC. He said that Peter Vaughn had been there and had insisted on seeing him and some of the others, and he wanted to know what I had told him. Then today, about an hour ago, Tom Henchy phoned again. He told me that Peter Vaughn had been murdered last night, and he asked me to say nothing to anyone about his having been at the ROCC yesterday. He said they had agreed that it would be inadvisable to mention it, and they didn't want me to. I said I would call him back, and I did, in a few minutes. During those few minutes what was mostly in my mind was what you said to us that night at Kanawha Spa. That was about murder too. I called him and told him I had decided I must tell you. He wanted me to come or meet him somewhere and discuss it, but I wouldn't. I came here. There it is. I hope to heaven . . ." He let it hang and left the chair. "I don't expect you to say anything, I don't want you to." He turned and was going, but Wolfe's voice stopped him.

"If you please! Who knows about this?"

"No one. I haven't told anybody, not even my wife."

"Not even about his coming to you?"

"No. And I won't. You must excuse me. It has been painful, telling you this. *Very* painful." He went.

I was on my feet, but Wolfe shook his head at me and I stayed put. My stepping to the hall for a look after the sound came of the front door closing was automatic, a habit ever since the day a bozo shut it from inside and stood near the open office door for half an hour, listening to us discuss his affairs.

I stepped back in. "Do I bother to sit?"

A corner of Wolfe's mouth was up. "You know, Archie, the most revealing manifestation of your self-esteem is not an action but an exclusion. You never crow. Nevertheless, accept my compliments."

"With pleasure. I won't deduct the twenty-two bucks. Do I sit down?"

"No. Bring them."

"Now?"

"Yes. Mr. Cramer might get to them at any moment."

"It's a quarter to three. Even if I deliver them in half an hour, which is doubtful, you can't possibly do them in forty-five minutes."

"I know I can't, confound it. I owe all this to that outlandish trip to Kanawha Spa."

"But you got the recipe for *saucisse minuit*."

"I did indeed. Bring them. Everyone Mr. Vaughn saw or spoke with, no exceptions. First ring Saul. We need him immediately."

As I went and started dialing, I was figuring whether it was the fourth time in history he had permitted his afternoon session with the orchids to be gummed up or only the third.

13

Maybe I seldom crow, and I'm all for self-esteem, but I have some flaws, and one of them showed when I walked into the office of the ROCC and crossed over to Maud Jordan at the switchboard and asked, "What time did Peter Vaughn get here yesterday morning?" That had been my suggestion to Wolfe just before Paul Whipple rang the doorbell, and using it verbatim appealed to one of my flaws, I'm not sure which one.

It wasn't answered. She looked down her long thin nose at me and asked, "Whom do you wish to see?"

I didn't press her, since Whipple had made it unnecessary. I told her Mr. Henchy, and it was urgent. She used the phone and told me to go on in, and as I went down the hall Harold R. Oster appeared in the doorway of the corner room. I would have preferred to have Henchy alone because lawyers always complicate things, but didn't make an issue of it. He didn't offer a hand, and neither did Henchy when Oster nodded me in and closed the door. Neither of them nodded me to a chair.

I said, standing, to Henchy at his desk, "Paul Whipple has told Nero Wolfe—not on the phone, in person—what he told you he would, about Peter Vaughn, and Mr. Wolfe wants to see you. Now. Everybody who spoke with Vaughn yesterday."

"Sit down," Oster said.

"I'd just have to get up again to go with you. You realize it's urgent. There's no telling how soon the cops will get here, and then you won't be available. If no one here knows where you've gone you won't be available to *them* for a while. If you think I'm pushing, I am."

Henchy started, "You certainly—" but Oster cut in, "I'll handle it, Tom. Keep your shirt on, Goodwin. If and when the police learn that Vaughn came here yesterday, we'll answer any questions they may care to ask. He merely wanted to inquire about Dunbar Whipple and Susan Brooke, how intimate they had been. He insisted on it and he was a damned nuisance. Nothing he said or did here could possibly have any connection with his murder. Tell Wolfe I'll see him later, at six o'clock, when *he's* available."

"He's available now." I focused on Henchy. "All right, I'll mention something that Mr. Wolfe would have preferred to mention himself, but it doesn't matter. Vaughn called me on the phone at ten minutes past five yesterday afternoon and said something that makes it extremely probable that he was murdered because of something that happened when he was here. Not only do Mr. Wolfe and I assume that, the cops do too."

"They don't know he was here." Oster.

"They'll find out, and it may not take them long. They know what Vaughn told me on the phone. What they assume is that his murder resulted from his contacts yesterday, and when they learn he was here—well. Talk about questions. The whole damn ROCC staff material witnesses. The bail—"

"Good God," Henchy blurted.

"I don't believe it," Oster said. "What did Vaughn tell you on the phone?"

"Mr. Wolfe may tell you. I won't."

"I don't believe it."

"Okay. It will be interesting to see who comes first, Homicide or the DA's bureau." I went to a chair and sat. "It will also be interesting to see how they handle it. Would you rather I wait outside?"

"Yes," Oster said. "We'll consider it."

"You'd better consider fast." I stood up. "I don't know how long Mr. Wolfe will hold on."

"I'm going." Henchy got to his feet. His pudgy cheeks were sagging. "I'm going to see him. You too, Harold."

"I want to consider it."

"No. I'm the responsible head of this organization. You come with me." Henchy moved.

"And the others," I said. "Everyone who spoke with Vaughn, even one word. Including Miss Jordan. Do you want to leave them here to deal with the cops if they come? With you not here?"

"No," Oster said. "Of course. If we go, Tom, they must go too. Wait in the anteroom, Goodwin."

"I advise you to step on it."

"We will. If we're going, the sooner the better."

I went. When I got to the anteroom Maud Jordan was busy on the phone, telling people to go to Henchy's room, and in a few minutes a girl came from inside, with very smooth dark skin and a little turned-up nose, to take over the switchboard, and Miss Jordan went inside. I decided to give them twenty

minutes for their huddle and then go in after them, and began exercising my neck by turning my head about ten times a
minute to look at the entrance door, hoping it wouldn't open.
It did once, and my belly muscles tightened, but it was only a
man with a package. Just one minute of the twenty was left
when I heard footsteps in the hall, and they came, Henchy in
the lead, then Oster, Cass Faison, Adam Ewing, Beth Tiger,
and Maud Jordan. No strangers.

Rising, I asked Henchy, "Miss Kallman?"

"She isn't here. She wasn't here yesterday." He turned to the
girl at the switchboard. "Miss Bowen, you don't know where
we're going."

"Well, I don't," she said.

"Also," I suggested, "you don't know my name, and if you're
asked to describe me you're not much good at describing
people."

"Do I describe him wrong?" she asked Henchy.

"Yes," Oster said. "Within reason."

I made another suggestion, that they go ahead and I would
take another elevator and also another taxi. You may think I
was overdoing it, but I knew darned well what would happen
the minute Cramer learned that Vaughn had gone there, if it
was still office hours. I was pleased to find that there was room
in my skull for still another suggestion, even though I had to
veto it—the suggestion that one of them, namely Miss Tiger,
might ride with me. It was nice to know that even in a crisis
I didn't totally exclude consideration of such matters as com-
panionship. I admit it was a factor that she had not yet given
the slightest indication that she was aware that I was human.

But I rode alone, and as my cab pulled up in front of the
old brownstone I was afraid there would be more delay. It was

five minutes past four, and it was at least even money that Wolfe had gone up to the plant rooms. Three of them were standing at the foot of the stoop steps, and the other three were climbing out of their taxi. I paid the hackie and went and led the way up, and as I reached the top the door was opened by Saul Panzer. "Mr. Henchy to the office," he told me, "and the others to the front room."

Lawyers can be pests and often are. Eight people in the end of that hall disposing of coats are a crowd, and when I got Henchy separated and started him down the hall to the office, there somehow was Oster, moving like a man who intends to stay in charge. I thought, What the hell, it will be simpler to use the connecting door, and let him come; and sure enough, he went straight to the red leather chair, stood in front of it, and told Wolfe, "Whipple's not here to interfere this time. You'll listen to *me*."

Relieved that Wolfe was there and my errand was done, I sat down and got my notebook and pen. Let him do the reacting.

He didn't crane to look up at Oster but focused on Henchy, who was in one of the yellow chairs Saul had moved up. "This is going to be unpleasant for all of us," he said. "Has Mr. Goodwin made the situation clear?"

Henchy nodded. "Clear enough so we're here. We came."

"You'll listen to me," Oster said, in charge. "We want to know what Vaughn said to Goodwin on the phone yesterday. What you *say* he said."

Wolfe slanted his head back. "Mr. Oster. I don't ask you to sit because I don't want you to. You will join the others in the front room. I am no longer acting in cooperation with you; henceforth my only commitment is to Mr. Paul Whipple. With me your status is now, to use a cant term, that of a murder suspect." He pointed. "That door."

Oster made a noise, part snort and part snarl. He sat. "That crap," he said. "The Great White Whosis. I'm a member of the bar, and what are you?"

Wolfe regarded him. "I really can't blame you. If I were a Negro I would have been locked up long ago—or I would be dead. You actually believe that your skin color and mine are factors in my treatment of you. Pfui. I'm not a troglodyte. Archie, the relevant portion of your telephone conversation with Mr. Vaughn yesterday afternoon."

I recited it for them as I had for Cramer, but slower and emphasizing "important," and adding at the end that he hadn't rung again. Henchy was frowning at me, concentrating. Oster was looking skeptical, but he was getting it. Wolfe spoke.

"Those were the last words, for us, from Mr. Vaughn. 'It's probably nothing.' But unfortunately for him it wasn't. It's a conclusion, more than an assumption, that he was going to see again someone he had seen earlier, or at least explore some suspicion resulting from an earlier contact. It's possible that that contact had not been at your office, but I know of none other he might have made relevant to the fate of Susan Brooke, and I doubt if the police do. It's also a conclusion, not lightly to be abandoned, that he was killed by the person who killed Miss Brooke. Do you reject that, Mr. Oster?"

"*Reject* it, no. *If* he said what Goodwin says he did."

"For me that is not moot. If it is for you, it will be a soliloquy. Are you willing to tell me what Mr. Vaughn said to you yesterday, and what you said to him?"

"He said nothing, and neither did I."

"He didn't see you?"

"He saw me, yes, but I exchanged no words with him. I was with Mr. Henchy in his room when Vaughn came, and I stayed and heard what they said, but I said nothing to Vaughn and he said nothing to me."

"Had you ever seen him before?"

"No."

"Had he ever seen you?"

"Not to my knowledge. I have been on television a few times."

"Did you see him again yesterday? After five o'clock?"

"No. Next question, where was I last evening? If you have a right to ask any questions at all, which I don't concede, you have a right to ask that. I'll answer it by saying that I can't produce witnesses for the entire evening and night. I wouldn't, for you, but anyway I couldn't."

"Few people could. Now, sir, I'm sure you would like this to be as brief as possible, and you can help. While I talk with Mr. Henchy you can explain to the others—"

"I'm staying right here."

"No. You're leaving, if not the house, the room. You—"

"I'm staying in this chair."

Wolfe's head turned. "Archie, you'll need Saul to help remove him; he's of a size. Since it must be done by force, put him out of the house."

"You wouldn't," Oster said.

I was up. "I have the build for it," I said, "but you'll be surprised to feel Saul Panzer in action. He's the Little White Whosis." I moved.

"Now wait a minute," Henchy said. "Harold, I don't like this. I don't think it's necessary." To Wolfe: "What were you going to say?"

"That Mr. Oster can describe the situation to the others, including what Mr. Vaughn said to Mr. Goodwin on the telephone. He can also learn if any of them have alibis—from eight o'clock last evening to two o'clock this morning—that can be verified." He turned to Oster. "Not difficult for a member of the bar."

I thought, He meant it, that their skin colors weren't factors. He was being as crusty with him as he would have been with a paleface. Oster thought he had something to say, first to Wolfe and then to Henchy, but apparently decided it would be more dignified to go without an exit line. A straight course to the connecting door to the front room would have taken him close to where I stood, and he made a point of circling wide. Also more dignified. When he was out and the door shut, I went back to my desk and notebook.

Wolfe said, "I'm obliged to you, Mr. Henchy. I don't like turmoil in my house."

The executive director nodded. "I don't like it anywhere. Many people wouldn't believe that, a man in my position, but I don't like it. I like restraint. I like peace, and maybe I'll get some before I die. I guess you want two things from me: what I said to Mr. Vaughn and where I was last evening."

"Not necessarily where you were, unless you have an alibi that can be established."

"I haven't, not for the whole time from eight o'clock to two. I know a little about alibis; I've had experience. As for Mr. Vaughn, I don't think I had ever seen him before. I see many people. I won't try to tell you what I said to him yesterday word for word because I'm not good at that. I didn't say much; it was really just one thing. Not about Susan's—Miss Brooke's —who killed her. He only asked about her and Dunbar, whether they were planning to marry. Of course I knew they were, but I didn't tell him that. I said I knew nothing about it, that I never meddled in the personal affairs of members of the staff. That's all there was to it."

"Can't you give me your exact words?"

He frowned and took five seconds. He shook his head. "I wouldn't want to try to. But it was just what I said. He wasn't with me more than four or five minutes. He wanted to see someone else, and I sent him to Mr. Faison."

"Why Mr. Faison?"

"Well, he insisted on seeing someone, and Susan had worked under him." Henchy's head turned for a glance at me and returned to Wolfe. "Tell me something. I know about your reputation. Is it possible that you honestly believe that one of us killed him? And killed Susan Brooke?"

"I think it likely, yes."

"Well, we didn't."

Wolfe nodded. "You would say that, naturally."

"Not just 'naturally.'" His hands were cupped over the ends of the chair arms, gripping them. "This is the truth if I ever spoke it, if anyone on our staff is a murderer I want him punished to the full extent. It will make it harder for us, it already has, Dunbar in jail, but if we expect to be treated like good citizens we must *be* good citizens. But you're wrong, I'm positive you're wrong. At noon today Mr. Ewing heard about the murder of Peter Vaughn on the radio and came and told me, and I got them in my room, all of them who spoke with Vaughn yesterday, and I put it to them straight. I told them the police might never learn that Vaughn had been there, but if they did, there was to be no covering up. I told them that if one of them was involved in any way, I wanted to know it then and there. I told them that if any one of them had the slightest suspicion about another one, he was to speak up, then and there."

He released the chair arms and turned his hands over. "I know my people, Mr. Wolfe. Not only because they're my color; I *know* them. In my position I have to. They were there in my room with me for nearly two hours, and we talked it out. When we got through I was absolutely certain that none of them was involved in the murder of Peter Vaughn or Susan Brooke, and I was certain that none of them had any suspicion of any of the others. I'm not saying I'm as good at it as you are, but I *know* them! Believe me, you're wrong. See them and question them, all right, but you're wrong!"

Wolfe wasn't impressed, and neither was I. The executive director of the ROCC had made a lot of speeches to a lot of audiences; he had had a lot of practice saying things like "This is the truth if I ever spoke it." Granting that he had spread the odds some on his own ticket, on the others he was merely taking the line that a man in his position had to take, though I admit he had done it better than some I had heard on other occasions.

"Admirable," Wolfe said. "I like to hear words well used. As for my being wrong, only the event can answer. Will you please ask Mr. Faison to come?"

"Certainly." Henchy levered on the chair arms to rise. "I was going to mention, about alibis. Of course I asked them. None of them has an alibi he could prove beyond question. Mr. Oster could have told you that, but he was agitated."

Wolfe nodded. "I like your taste in words. 'Agitated.' He was indeed."

I was at the door to the front room, and when I swung it open as Henchy came, the sound of Oster's voice, in charge, was heard. It didn't stop, so apparently Henchy summoned Faison by hand; anyhow, the fund raiser appeared and crossed to the chair his boss had vacated as I shut the door.

Wolfe scowled at him, and no wonder. What was there left to ask? Cass Faison's grin wasn't working, and from his expression it seemed doubtful if it would ever work again, but his coal-black skin still had its high gloss when the light hit it right.

Wolfe spoke. "No preamble is required, Mr. Faison, since Mr. Oster has described the situation. Mr. Henchy sent Mr. Vaughn to you?"

Faison nodded. "That's right."

"To your room?"

"Yes."

"Were you alone with him?"

"Yes."

"Had you ever seen him before?"

"No. None of us had ever seen him before."

"How long was he with you?"

"Not more than three or four minutes. I wasn't timing it. Possibly five."

"What was said?"

"He said the same thing to all of us. He wanted to know how intimate Miss Brooke had been with Mr. Whipple. We all said the same thing to him. We said we didn't know. He didn't want to believe that. He said someone there must know. He was all—he was in a fret. I sent him to Mr. Ewing."

Wolfe's lips were tight. He turned to me. "This is farcical."

"Yes, sir. They talked it out for two hours with Mr. Henchy."

"Bring them."

It occurred to me as I crossed to the door that I might as well get a little personal satisfaction. I would put Miss Tiger in the red leather chair. But Wolfe might himself interfere

with that, so when I opened the door I asked Henchy to come
and took him to the red leather chair, and then summoned
the others. Since Saul had moved up enough chairs for all, I
was free to enjoy the look on Oster's face when he saw I had
foxed him. That settled my relations with Harold R. Oster.
We were enemies for life, and that suited me fine.

Wolfe took them in, from Henchy at the far left to Maud
Jordan at the far right, nearest me. "I'm through," he said. "I'm
through with you for today, but not with the job I'm doing.
The situation is unaltered. I have learned nothing whatever
from Mr. Henchy, Mr. Oster, or Mr. Faison, except that you are
presenting a solid front. You are maintaining that your exchanges with Mr. Vaughn yesterday were identical. I don't
believe it. I believe—"

"I'm not!" It was Maud Jordan.

Wolfe's eyes went to her. "Not what, Miss Jordan?"

"What you said about identical exchanges. I know what that
man, Vaughn, asked the rest of them, but he didn't ask me
anything. He merely said he wanted to see Mr. Henchy."

"When he entered."

"Yes."

"And gave you his name."

"Of course."

"And when he departed?"

"He didn't say anything." She upped her chin and a half.
"I want to say something *now*. You're hounding these people,
and I think it's outrageous. You're bullying them just because
they're Negroes. And who are you? Where were *you* born?"

She was only the switchboard, but nobody shushed her, not
even a murmur or two. She was a volunteer, and she had given
half a grand to the fund for Medgar Evers's children. Wolfe's

head turned left. "Do you wish to support that indictment, Mr. Henchy?"

"No. I think you're wrong, but no, I wouldn't call it bullying."

"Do you wish to add anything, Miss Jordan?"

"No. I mean what I said."

"Mr. Ewing, I haven't spoken with you. Have you anything to say?"

"No, only that I agree with Mr. Henchy. If you think one of us is a murderer, you're wrong, but I wouldn't call it bullying. I know what it will be like if the police find out he came there yesterday morning. Are you going to tell them?"

"Miss Tiger. Do you wish to say anything?"

"No," she said, barely audible.

"Then we're through. For today. I may see all of you again, and I certainly expect to see one of you; I would give something to know which one. To answer Mr. Ewing's question, I shall not tell the police of Mr. Vaughn's ill-fated visit. I bid you good afternoon merely as a civility." He leaned back, laced his fingers at his center mound, and closed his eyes.

I was surprised at Oster. Not a word. He got up and headed for the hall. Saul Panzer, who was on a chair over by the bookshelves, followed him out, and as the others rose and moved, no one saying anything, I stayed put. Saul was there. I don't especially mind holding a coat for a murderer, but I like to know when I'm doing it. I looked at my watch: 5:19. Wolfe could still have forty minutes with the orchids, but apparently he preferred to take a nap. I sat and watched his big chest rise and fall, expecting, and I admit hoping, to see the lip exercise start, but it didn't. When the sounds from the hall ended with the closing of the front door and Saul came and took the yellow chair nearest me, he was still just sitting and breathing.

"In a way," I told Saul, "I'm glad you've seen her. I'll be doing a lot of talking about her in the future and you'll appreciate
it better. I'm sure you'll agree that the best way to handle it is
to cherish and covet her at a distance, but the question is what
distance. A mile is a distance, but so is a yard or even an inch.
I wish I knew more about poetry. If I could turn out—"

"Shut up!" Wolfe bellowed.

I turned and said, "Yes, sir. I was only remarking about the
one single aspect of the party that struck me as worthy of remark. Was there any other?"

"No." He had straightened up.

"Then there's no argument. I might as well go on remarking
about Miss Tiger. Two days ago I said there wasn't one sensible
thing anybody could do. Now it's even worse; there's not even
one unsensible thing."

"Confound it, don't sit there inventing grotesque words!"

"Shall I go?" Saul asked.

"No. When Archie exhausts inanity he may have a suggestion. I won't. It's hopeless. Whatever Vaughn saw or heard
there yesterday is buried beyond recovery. One of those six
people either killed him or knows who did, but that key to his
identity is undiscoverable. There's another one somewhere, but
a hundred men might not find it in a hundred days. Saul?"

"I'm sorry."

"Archie?"

"Sorry and sad."

He glared. "Two highly trained and highly skilled men, and
what good are you? Go somewhere. Do something. Am I to sit
here another evening, and go up to bed, contemplating frus-
tration? Reflecting, in desperation, as I did day before yesterday, on a diphthong?"

Saul and I exchanged glances. Our genius was going potty on us. To humor him I inquired, "A diphthong?"

"Yes. Tenuous almost to nullity, it was unworthy of consideration. It still is. But I'm bereft, and it's a fact. Get Mr. Vaughn."

For half a second I thought he was worse than potty; then, realizing that there was a Mr. Vaughn who was still alive, and that diphthongs might be his hobby, I got at the phone. With his son not yet buried, Samuel Vaughn probably wouldn't be at Heron Manhattan, Inc., but I tried it on the chance, was told that he wasn't in today, and dialed his home number. He wasn't accessible until I made it clear that Nero Wolfe wanted to ask him a question—I didn't say about a diphthong—and in a couple of minutes I had him, and Wolfe took his phone.

"I presume to disturb you, Mr. Vaughn, only because I am concerned with the death of your son in connection with my investigation of the death of Susan Brooke, and I need a bit of information you may be able to supply. According to the published accounts, your son graduated from Harvard in nineteen fifty-nine. Is that correct?"

"Yes. Why do you ask?"

"To lead to the next question. I'd rather not elucidate now, but it's possible that this will be helpful in identifying a murderer. Do you know if your son was acquainted with a fellow student named Richard Ault? A-U-L-T. Perhaps a classmate?"

"I'm afraid I don't— Wait a minute . . . yes, I do. That was the name of the boy that committed suicide that summer, after they graduated. My son told me about it. Yes, he knew him rather well; they took the same courses. But I don't understand . . . what possible connection . . ."

"There may be none. If I find one, you'll understand then.

Do you know if your son ever visited Richard Ault at his home —perhaps at vacation time?"

"Where was his home?"

"Evansville, Indiana."

"Then he didn't. I'm sure he didn't. Have you any reason to think he did?"

"No. I'm obliged to you, Mr. Vaughn, for indulging me. If this leads to anything, the obligation will be canceled."

As I cradled the receiver my eyes were narrowed at it. I was considering diphthongs. Ch? Gh? Au? Wh? Br? I'd have to look it up. Too many years had passed since the fourth grade, or maybe fifth. I was interrupted by Wolfe saying, "Get Mr. Drucker."

Again it took me half a second to catch up; it had been ten days since I had eaten roast beef and apple pie with Otto Drucker, the distinguished citizen, in my hotel room in Racine. I got his number from the file and put in the call, and when I got him I took time for a few sociable remarks before passing him to Wolfe. He told Wolfe it was a pleasure to speak with a man whose career he had followed with interest and admiration.

Wolfe grunted. "I may forfeit the admiration by the job I'm on now. You may be able to supply some needed information. I suppose you remember your conversation with Mr. Goodwin?"

"Certainly. Susan Brooke. Are you still on that?"

"I am. I'm floundering. What can you tell me of the young man who shot himself on the porch of the Brooke house?"

"Not much. I told Goodwin all I know. I don't even remember his name."

"His name was Richard Ault. Do you know if any member

of his family came to Racine? Or any representative of the family?"

"I don't know, but I don't think so. As far as I recollect, they held the body here only a day or two and shipped it. I don't remember that anyone came to get it. I can find out."

"It isn't worth the trouble. I believe Mr. Goodwin has told you to command us if at any time you need information from here."

"He didn't say 'command,' but he said you'd reciprocate and I appreciate it. I like that 'command.' If you need more on this let me know."

Wolfe said he would, hung up, pushed the phone away as if he resented it, which he does, pushed his chair back, left it, walked over to the globe, twirled it, and focused on a spot near the center of the United States of America.

In a minute he demanded, not turning, "Where the devil is Evansville?"

"If you've got Indiana, at the bottom, on the Ohio River."

Another ten seconds, and he turned. "How do you get there?"

"Probably the quickest would be a plane to Louisville."

"I'd have to be back Monday morning for a little job," Saul said.

"No, Archie will go. You're needed here. Archie, find—"

He stopped because I had turned to the phone and started dialing.

14

At ten minutes past two Friday morning I sat on a wooden chair at the end of a glass-topped desk in a room with two windows, being sized up by a cop. I wasn't exactly in the pink, after the day in New York, the plane ride to Louisville, and the three-hour drive in a rented car to Evansville, but since I now knew which diphthong it was, and I would sleep better after I got the answers to a few questions, and police headquarters is open all night, I had stopped at the hotel only long enough to sign in. I admit that as I sat I had to tell myself to keep my shoulders up.

The cop's name was Sievers, Lieutenant Sievers, an old pro with very little hair but plenty of jaw. He gave my New York State detective license a thorough look, handed it back, and frowned at me. "Archie Goodwin," he said. "Haven't I seen that name somewhere?"

"I hope not on a hot dodger. You may have seen the name of the man I work for, Nero Wolfe."

"Oh." He nodded. "That one. Yeah. How do you stand him?"

"I've asked myself that question a thousand times, and damned if I can answer it."

"Don't expect me to. What's your problem here?"

"Just a little information we need, about a man named Richard Ault, or I should say his family. He's dead. He committed suicide in Racine, Wisconsin, on August fourteenth, nineteen fifty-nine."

"Yeah, I know."

"This was his home town, wasn't it?"

"It was. He was born here."

"Did you know him?"

"I knew him by sight. I don't know if I ever spoke to him. He wasn't the kind we have to speak to much. Why are you interested in him now?"

"We're not, in him. A point has come up in a case we're on that his family might know about. I'll see them tomorrow—I mean today—but I thought it wouldn't hurt to find out what they're like first. How do they stand locally?"

"They don't stand. You won't see them tomorrow. There's no one to see."

"No one at all?"

"No. If you want details, Richard Ault's father, Benjamin Ault, Junior, had a furniture factory, a big one. He inherited it from *his* father, Benjamin Senior. Benjamin Junior died about ten years ago. Let's see . . ." He shut his eyes and lowered his head. He looked up. "That's right, nineteen fifty-three. You don't believe in making notes, huh? Out here we always make notes."

"So do I when they may be needed. What about brothers or sisters?"

He shook his head. "Richard was an only."

"There's still Mrs. Ault. Where is she?"

"I don't know, and I don't know who does. There's a lawyer who might named Littauer, H. Ernest Littauer. He handled it when she sold the factory."

I had my notebook out and was scribbling. When in Evansville do as the Romans do. "I need all the dope I can get," I said. "Am I keeping you from anything important?"

"Hell no. Not until the phone rings to report a hit and run."

"I hope it won't. When did Mrs. Ault sell the factory?"

"About three years ago. When Benjamin Junior died, her husband, she changed the name of the business to M. and R. Ault, Inc. M for Marjorie and R for Richard. Then a couple of years after Richard's death she sold it and left town. As far as I know she has never been back, and I don't know where she is. You do shorthand, huh?"

"I guess you could call it that to be polite. I understand Richard went to Harvard University."

"I believe he did. Let's see." In a moment: "Yes, he did."

"Do you happen to know if his mother ever went to visit him there?"

He cocked his head and eyed me. "You know, maybe I'm not as sharp as you are, out here in the sticks, but I can count up to ten. A point in a case his family might know about, nuts. Suppose you open up a little, huh?"

I nodded. "I intend to, but I wasn't being sharp. If you had told me she's here in Evansville I wouldn't even have bothered to take a look at her. I'm about done. Did she ever visit him at Harvard?"

"I don't know, but it would be a good bet. He was the apple of her eye."

I took a breath. "Now. I hate to ask it. I'm afraid to ask it, but here goes. Describe her."

"I thought so," he said.

"I only hope you'll still think so after you describe her."

"Well, three years ago, about a hundred and forty pounds. Late forties or early fifties. Five feet six. Light brown hair with a little gray. Brown eyes, a little close. Not much of a mouth. Long narrow nose, extra narrow. Not exactly a double chin, but a crease in it. That enough?"

"I'm not much at paying compliments," I said, "but you are absolutely the best describer south of the North Pole. I could have saved wear and tear on my nerves by asking for it sooner. One more question. Would you care to take a trip to New York this morning, expenses paid and honored guest treatment?"

"You're damn right I would. But I'm an employee of the city of Evansville. What have you got on Mrs. Ault?"

"You're an officer of the law, dedicated to the service of justice, and you're needed to identify a murderer—a double murderer. I'm sticking my neck out. If you call the New York Police Department and spill it, my name is mud, and I doubt if you'll be needed. If you come with me, justice will be served just as well or better, you can hang around a day or two if you care to, and if you like to see your picture in the paper, the *Gazette* has a circulation over a million. Of course if Evansville couldn't manage even for an hour without you . . ."

"You don't have to clown it, Goodwin. Is this straight, Marjorie Ault is a murderer?"

"My neck's out far enough."

"When are you leaving?"

"There's a plane from Louisville at five p.m. I have a car I rented there. I'd like to ask that lawyer, Littauer, a couple of questions." I stood. "How long have you been on the force?"

"Twenty-six years."

"Then what the hell, you don't have to spell your name. I would deeply appreciate it if you'd leave the monkey wrench in the drawer. Say we leave at one-thirty?"

He wasn't sure, he would ring me around noon, but from the look in his eye and the grip in his hand as we shook I was satisfied that I would have a companion for the trip home.

It was exactly three o'clock when, after leaving a call for seven-forty-five, I got between sheets in the hotel room, and I certainly needed a nap, but there was something on my mind. Not whether it was in the bag, that was okay, but how we got it. Had it been luck or genius or what? It had been years since I had given up trying to figure how Wolfe's mind worked, but this was special. I hadn't happened to notice that there was an au in four of the names: Paul, Ault, Maud, and Vaughn, but I might have; anybody might. That was nothing special. The point was, if I *had* noticed it, then what? I would have filed it as just coincidence, and probably Wolfe had too. But although filed, that au in four of the names was still somewhere in his mind later, when it got really tough, so in going over and over it, every detail and every factor, that popped up. Okay, but then what? Did he deliberately team them up?

Paul and Ault
Paul and Maud
Paul and Vaughn
Ault and Maud
Ault and Vaughn
Maud and Vaughn

Then did he consider each pair and finally decide that the one that might not be just coincidence was Ault and Maud, because if a woman named Ault changed her name she might pick one that had au in it? No. I could have done that myself. I hadn't, but I could. What had happened in his mind that had made him phone Samuel Vaughn and Otto Drucker, and send me to Evansville, was something that had never happened in mine and never would. He had said "tenuous almost to nullity." But there I was in Evansville, and I knew who had killed Susan Brooke and Peter Vaughn, and probably I never would have known if Wolfe hadn't started reflecting on a diphthong. Reflecting that I had been wasting some precious time, I turned over to go to sleep, but jor butted in. She had not only used the Ault au in Maud, she had also used the Marjorie jor in Jordan. If Wolfe had known Mrs. Ault's name was Marjorie he would have sewed it up a week ago. On that I slept.

I had left a call for 7:45 because on 35th Street it would be 8:45 and I wanted to get Wolfe before he went up to the plant rooms. I did. Fritz answered and relayed it to Wolfe's room, and his voice came, gruff.

"Yes?"

"Me. I've had four hours' sleep and I need more, so I'll make it brief. If I talked for an hour you'd like every word of it. Wrapped up. Not a single snag. Reserve a room at the Churchill for Mr. George Sievers." I spelled it. "He'll arrive around eight-thirty this evening and so will I. Tell Fritz not to keep my dinner warm; I'll eat with Sievers on the plane."

"Are there any relatives in Evansville?"

"No. She's alone in the world, as she told you."

He grunted. "Very satisfactory." He hung up.

Sometimes I think he overdoes it. I admit everything had been said that needed saying, but he might at least have asked how the weather was or if my bed was all right. It was. I rolled over and went back to sleep.

It wasn't absolutely essential to see H. Ernest Littauer, and I don't know when I would have moved again if the phone hadn't rung. As I reached for it I glanced at my wrist: 10:42. It was Lieutenant Sievers. He said he had fixed it to go, and there was an hour's difference between Evansville and Louisville, so we should roll by one o'clock to make the five-o'clock plane. I made it to my feet with the help of a healthy groan and headed for the bathroom.

Perhaps the trouble with my experiences with lawyers is that I am never a prospective client, ready with a checkbook for a retainer. All I ever have is questions, usually questions they would prefer not to answer, and so it was with H. Ernest Littauer, in a big sunny room with a fine view of the Ohio River. I merely wanted to know if he had been in communication with Mrs. Marjorie Ault during the past year or so, and he merely didn't want to tell me. And he didn't, but I gathered that he had no idea where she was and didn't care.

When I got to the parking lot at a quarter to one, Sievers was already there, with a suitcase big enough to last at least a week, and I suspected I had been a little too hospitable. It wasn't going to be billed to a client. But he was going to help clean up the mess, so he was welcome. He was good enough company, though not in the class of Otto Drucker. By the time we touched concrete at Idlewild—I mean Kennedy International Airport—it was obvious that he was only a good working cop, which was why after twenty-six years he was still a lieutenant. He said he preferred to handle his evening himself if he wasn't needed, so I taxied him to the Churchill and proceeded to 35th Street.

It was only eight-forty, but Wolfe was in the office with coffee, and that deserved a grin. Business was not to be mentioned at meals, so he had either started dinner early or speeded it up in order to be away from the table when I arrived. There was a hint of feeling in his look and voice as he greeted me, as there always is when I return safe and sound from a trip in long-distance machines. I stood in the middle of the rug and took a good stretch, and said, "My God, it's cold around here, much colder than down on the Ohio River. The warmth in this room is wonderful, even if I had no personal connection with its production. I admit that the rapid advance of automation may result—"

"Sit down and report!"

I did so, verbatim. He didn't lean back and shut his eyes; there was no need to, since it was only the happy ending. When I finished by saying that we might be stuck for a week in town by Lieutenant Sievers he didn't bat an eye.

He picked up his coffee cup and emptied it and put it down. "Archie," he said, "I tender my apologies. I noticed that confounded diphthong Monday evening, and I could have sent you to Evansville then. Three wretched days."

"Yeah. Well, you finally got around to it. I accept the apology. It's too bad it's Friday night, the weekend, and some of them may not be available tomorrow, maybe none of them. I suggest that they deserve to be present, all the ROCC crowd, even Oster. Also Mr. and Mrs. Kenneth Brooke. And why not Susan's mother? In a way, her more than anyone else. She was there in the house with Susan when Richard Ault shot himself on the porch. According to Drucker, she helped Susan give him the boot. She ought to—"

I stopped short.

Wolfe asked, "What?"

"Nothing. But that's what you thought about the diphthong: it wasn't worth considering. What if she decided to get the mother too and picked tonight for it? That would be just great."

I swiveled. I didn't have Mrs. Matthew Brooke's number on the card and had to look in the book. I got it, and dialed, and sat and listened to fourteen buzzes, two more than my usual allowance. I don't dial wrong numbers, so I didn't try again but dialed another number, one that was on the card, and that time got an answer, a voice that I recognized, saying, "Mrs. Brooke's residence."

"This is Archie Goodwin," I said, "at Nero Wolfe's office. Mr. Wolfe wants to ask Mrs. Matthew Brooke a question, and I just dialed her number and got no answer. I thought she might be with you. Is she?"

"No. What does he want to ask her?"

"Nothing very important, just a routine question, but it would help to have the answer now. Do you know where I can get her?"

"No, I don't. But it's odd. . . ."

Silence. After five seconds of it I asked, "What's odd?"

"I thought perhaps— Where are you?"

"Nero Wolfe's office."

"She isn't there?"

"No."

"I thought perhaps it was him she was going to see. She phoned about an hour ago and asked to use my car—she often does—and she said she was going to see someone who could tell her something about Susan, and I asked her if it was Nero

Wolfe, and she wouldn't say. She said she had promised not
to. Are you sure—"

"And she took the car?"

"I suppose so, of course. Have you—"

"The blue sedan?"

"Yes. Have you—"

"Sorry, I'm being interrupted." I hung up and turned. "As
I said, just great. About an hour ago Mrs. Matthew Brooke
took Mrs. Kenneth Brooke's car to go to meet someone who
had phoned her that she could tell her something about Susan.
She may still be alive. Of all the lousy breaks. Do I talk to
Cramer or do you?"

"What for?"

"For God's sake! A stop-and-take on the goddam car!"

"It isn't necessary. Saul."

"What do you mean, Saul? He can't—"

"He is covering Miss Jordan. As you know, he was told yesterday to inquire about her. He telephoned this morning
shortly after you had reported from Evansville, and I told him
to get Fred and Orrie and keep her under constant surveil-
lance."

I returned to my pocket the key ring I had got out. Its col-
lection included the key to the locked drawer from which I
had been going to get the license number of the blue sedan.
"Damn it, you might have told me."

"That's querulous, Archie."

"If that means peevish, I am. How would you feel or I feel
or Cramer feel if she added another one to the list after we had
her tagged? And you realize that any dimwit can lose a tail,
even if it's Saul Panzer. You'd like to deliver her wrapped up,
sure, so would I. But it would be nearly as good and a lot safer
to ring him now and say the woman who killed Susan Brooke

and Peter Vaughn is now somewhere in your territory in a blue Heron sedan with Mrs. Matthew Brooke and is going to kill her. The car's number is here in the drawer."

He called me. He asked, merely wanting information, "Do you wish to do that?"

"Of course I don't wish to!"

"Would Saul?"

"If he has lost her, yes. If he's still on her, no."

He turned a palm up. "Then it's simple. We determine our action or inaction by the extent of our confidence in Saul's craft and sagacity. Mine, though not infinite, is considerable, and he knows she has killed two people. Yours?"

"I don't have to tell you. When did he last call in?"

"At twenty minutes past six, from a booth on Lexington Avenue. She was in the building where she lives. Fred and Orrie had followed her there from the building where she works, and Saul had relieved Fred at six o'clock. He had—"

The doorbell rang.

I went to the hall for a look, swallowed something that had been wanting to be swallowed for ten minutes, turned my head, and said, "Mr. Panzer and Miss Jordan. Have they an appointment?"

15

As I approached I saw through the one-way glass that Saul
had a hold on her right arm, so as I opened the door I was prepared to take her left one if necessary, but she crossed the
sill without any help. Saul said, "Orrie's in the car with Mrs.
Brooke. Do you want her?" I said no, Orrie had better see her
home, and he went to tell him. I mentioned somewhere that
I don't mind helping a murderer with a coat, but Maud Jordan
shook her head when I offered. She was keeping it on. Thinking that Saul should have the honor of escorting her to the
office, I waited until he came back in and then followed them.
Saul moved up one of the yellow chairs for her and started
for one for himself, but Wolfe told him to take the red leather.
Before he did so he took an object from his pocket and put it
on Wolfe's desk, and Wolfe made a face at it and told me to
take it. It was a snub-nosed Haskell .32, and I took a look to

see if it was loaded. It was, and I dropped it in a drawer. Saul said, "It was in her coat pocket," and sat.

She hadn't opened her mouth. She did now, and spoke to the point. "I haven't got a permit for that gun," she said. "That's against the law, having a gun without a permit, but it doesn't justify this kind of treatment." Her eyes darted to Saul and back to Wolfe. "I was getting into a car at the invitation of the woman driving it, and that man assaulted me."

Wolfe ignored her and asked Saul, "Should you report?"

He shook his head. "I don't think it's necessary, unless you want the details, where and when. We closed in when she opened the car door and was getting in, and I put her in the back seat with me, and Orrie got in front with Mrs. Brooke. That's all there was to it. There was no commotion. Mrs. Brooke made a little noise, but we calmed her down. Orrie's good at that. It was in Central Park. Do you want details?"

"Not now. Probably never." Wolfe turned. "This need not be prolonged, Mrs. Ault. Since it can easily be—"

"My name is Maud Jordan."

"So it is. There's nothing immutable about a name. A man's name is whatever he chooses to call himself. If you resent being addressed by your former name, Marjorie Ault, I'll refer to it—"

"My name has always been Maud Jordan."

"That won't do. There's a man at the Churchill Hotel, my guest, who arrived about an hour ago. Lieutenant Sievers, George Sievers, of the Evansville police. If he isn't immediately available he will be shortly. Shall we postpone the conversation until Mr. Goodwin brings him?"

I have seen a lot of faces do a lot of things, but what hers did in twenty seconds, maybe a little more, was amazing. When she heard the name, Sievers, her eyes shut, tight, and I swear

I could see the color go from her skin, though I wouldn't have said, before, that it had any color. I don't often get fancy, but it was exactly as if what I saw going was not color, but life. It wasn't like just turning pale; it was quite different. I didn't enjoy it. I looked at Saul and saw that he was seeing it too, and he wasn't enjoying it either.

In another half a minute her eyes opened, at Wolfe, but I had her in profile and couldn't see if they had changed too. "George Sievers was in my class at school," she said.

Apparently she thought that called for comment. Wolfe grunted.

"Anyway," she said, "I can talk. You don't know how hard it's been. The niggers. Sometimes I thought I would choke, with Mr. Henchy and Mr. Ewing and Mister Mister Mister. But I did it, I killed her. She had a right to die, and I killed her."

"I advise you, Miss Jordan, not to—"

"My name is Marjorie Ault!"

"As you will. I advise you not to speak until you are more composed."

"I haven't been as composed for years as I am now. Since the day my Richard died. I'm glad you found out about me because now I can talk. I thought you would. Do you know when I thought you would?"

"No."

"The day I was here with the niggers, the first time, when you asked so much about the phone call, about it being Susan's voice. I thought you knew then that she hadn't made the call, that nobody had, that there hadn't been any phone call. Didn't you?"

"No. If I had . . ." Wolfe let it go. No use trying to explain when she wanted only to talk, not listen.

She talked. "I knew someday I would be telling about it, but I didn't know it would be you. I want you to know, I want everybody to know, that I didn't decide to kill her just on account of my Richard. All I decided was that I wanted to see her, to know about her. That's why I sold the business and— You know I had a good business?"

"Yes."

"That's why I sold it and got it all in cash and came to New York and changed my name. But after I got here I saw it wouldn't be so easy because I didn't want to be *friends* with her. Then when she started working for that ROCC, that was my chance. I had plenty of money, and I made a big contribution and offered to work for them. That was hard, I want you to understand that, and I want you to understand that up till then I didn't intend to kill her. I didn't have any idea of killing her. I didn't even want to hurt her; I just wanted to *know* her. Do you understand that?"

"Yes."

"Do you understand how hard it was, there with *them*?"

"Yes."

"I want to be sure you do. I had had some niggers working in my factory, sweeping floors, that kind. I'll see if you understand. Why did I decide to kill her?"

"That's obvious. Because she was going to marry a Negro."

She nodded. "You do. My Richard wasn't good enough for her, she and her mother had driven my Richard out of their house, to kill himself there on their porch, and she was going to marry a nigger. It came to me in a funny way. She was always talking about civil rights, all she cared about was civil rights, and now she was going to marry a nigger. Then she had a right, she had a right to die, so I decided to kill her. Won't everybody understand that?"

"Certainly. Especially Negroes. It may be more difficult to understand why you killed Peter Vaughn. Did he recognize you when he came there Wednesday morning?"

"He thought he did but wasn't sure. He had seen me twice, years ago, when I went to see my Richard at college. They were classmates. On his way out he asked me some questions, and my answers didn't satisfy him, and I arranged to meet him that evening."

"To kill him."

She frowned. "I don't think so."

"You took the gun along."

She passed her tongue over her lips. "I'm not going to talk about that."

"And you had it again this evening, for Mrs. Brooke. The same gun?"

"Of course. It was my husband's. He always carried it when he brought money from the bank for the payroll. I don't want to talk about that, I want to talk about Susan. She called me Maud, you know, and I called her Susan. Of course my Richard had called her Susan, he told me all about her, but I had never met her. I have two pictures of her that he had, one with him. I'm not sure you understand how I felt about her. I'm not saying I loved her because my Richard had, that wasn't it exactly, but I wanted to be close to her, I wanted to see her every day. Do you understand that?"

"I think I do. It's somewhat involved." Wolfe's eyes moved. "The kitchen extension, Archie."

I pressed a button and got up and went. As I passed Saul he winked. I'm going to talk him out of that some day. In the kitchen I sat at my breakfast table, pulled the phone over, and dialed. Cramer doesn't like to be called at his home number, but if I had rung Homicide South I would probably have got

Rowcliff, and I didn't want to take the time and trouble to get him stuttering. After four buzzes a female voice I knew said hello, and I said, "This is Archie Goodwin, Mrs. Cramer. May I speak to the inspector, please?"

She said she'd see, and in a minute there was a growl in my ear, "What do you want, Goodwin?"

"I'm in the kitchen. Mr. Wolfe needs help. The woman who killed Susan Brooke and Peter Vaughn is in the office with him, talking a blue streak, and won't stop. She has explained why she killed Susan, and now she's explaining—"

"Damn you, are you clowning?"

"I am not. I'm sick and tired of being accused of clowning by cops. This morning in Evansville, Indiana, a police lieutenant did, and I brought him—"

"Who's the woman with Wolfe?"

"I'd rather not mention names on the phone. Another thing, the gun she shot Vaughn with is in my desk drawer and I haven't got a permit for it. I don't like—"

"Is this straight, Goodwin?"

"You know damn well it is. As Dolly Brooke would say, are I crazy? Would I—"

The connection went. I went to a shelf for a glass and to the refrigerator for milk. It would probably be six or seven minutes before company came, and I had had enough of that face, even in profile.

16

Yesterday afternoon Paul Whipple came, no appointment, a little after six o'clock. He was quite natty in a brown macron or zacron or something, tropical weight, about the same shade as his skin, but I thought he was rushing it a little. It was toward the end of May, but it was cool and breezy, and on my morning walk I had buttoned my jacket and wanted more. I took him to the office and to the red leather chair, and Wolfe, who had just picked up his current book, put it down almost politely. They conversed a little on matters of interest, such as the trial of Marjorie Ault, which had just ended with a conviction and a life sentence, and then Whipple mentioned what he had come to mention.

"I was wondering," he said, "about a check I sent you six weeks ago. It hasn't come through my bank, and I was wondering if you got it."

Wolfe nodded. "I tore it up."

"But you shouldn't. I'm going to insist. It wasn't much, for what you did, but I said we would pay what we could, and we want to. My wife and my son—we insist."

"I resent that, Mr. Whipple."

"You *resent* it?"

"Certainly. I undertook to cancel an obligation, and I have done so, and you would restore it. Pfui. I wouldn't have made the original fantastic engagement, to find a blemish on that woman, for any fee any man could offer. Its development wasn't your doing and didn't affect the nature of my commitment. What you insist on is keeping me in your debt."

"That's sophistry."

"Good. Probably no man will ever corral truth, but Protagoras came closer to it than Plato. If you send me another check I'll burn it. Your son sent me a well-worded letter of appreciation, and it was welcome. How is he?"

"He's all right. This was a hard experience for him, but he's all right. He's developing another—uh—personal interest. You probably remember her, with your memory. Beth Tiger. A very attractive girl."

Wolfe shot a glance at me, and I let my jaw fall, but not in time. Whipple was going on. "My wife likes her and she's very happy about it. I'm going to tell you something my wife said the other day. We were discussing the trial, Mrs. Ault, and we got to talking about you, and she said, 'I wish he was a Negro.'" He smiled. "Now *there's* a compliment."

Wolfe grunted. "If I were, Mr. Goodwin would have to be one too."

I haven't bothered to take that apart. As I said, I gave up long ago trying to figure how his mind works.